PIRATE ISLAND

Another You Say Which Way Adventure
by:

BLAIR POLLY & DM POTTER

FAIRYTALE
FACTORY

ISBN-13: 978-1518784941

ISBN 10: 1518784941

How This Book Works

- This story depends on YOU.

- YOU say which way the story goes.

- What will YOU do?

At the end of each chapter, you get to make a decision. Turn to the page that matches your choice. **P62** means turn to page 62.

There are many paths to try. You can read them all over time. Right now, it's time to start the story. Good luck finding the treasure.

Oh … and watch out for sharks!

Pirate Island

At the Resort.

Your family is on holiday at a lush tropical island resort in the Caribbean. But you're not in the mood to sit around the pool with the others, you want to go exploring. You've heard that pirate treasure's been found in these parts and you're keen to find some too. You put a few supplies into your daypack, fill your drinking bottle with water, grab your mask and snorkel, and head towards the beach.

You like swimming, but you've been planning this treasure hunt for months and now is as good a time as any to start. The beach outside the resort stretches off in both directions.

To your right it runs past the local village, where children laugh as they splash and play in the water. Palm trees line the shore and brightly colored fishing boats rest on the sand above the high tide mark. Past the village, way off in the distance, is a lighthouse.

To your left, the sandy beach narrows quickly and soon becomes a series of rocky outcrops jutting into the sea. Steep cliffs rise up from the rocky shore to meet the stone walls of an old and crumbling fortress.

You have four hours before your family expects you back. Which way should you go?

It is time to make your first decision. Do you:

Go right and head towards the lighthouse? **P3**

Or

Go left and head towards the rocks and the old fortress?

P9

You have chosen to go right and head towards the lighthouse.

After deciding to turn right and walk out to the lighthouse you make your way down to the hard, wet sand where the walking will be easier.

Off in the distance, past the local village, the palm trees gradually thin out and the lush vegetation gives way to low sand dunes, scrub, and hardy grasses. A narrow sand spit, with a lighthouse on its far end, juts out into the ocean. The spit curves around in a gentle arc, forming a protected bay sheltered from the full force of the ocean beyond. Seabirds dive into the bay's sparkling blue waters as they hunt for fish.

As you walk down the beach, you pass resort guests lying on beach towels, swimming in the ocean, and playing games in the sand. You're not interested in all that, you want to find treasure.

You're pretty sure there is unlikely to be any treasure so close to civilization, so you pick up the pace. You want to get as far away from the others as you can and check out the windswept sand spit where it's far more likely you'll find treasure. What clever pirate would bury his treasure so close to the village?

Coconut palms line the shoreline and you hear birds and other animals in the jungle beyond the trees. Out in the bay, small fish are leaping out of the water trying to escape bigger fish below. Hungry gulls dive bomb the little fish from above. Then, a moment later, even bigger fish are leaping from the water and you wonder what is chasing them. You've never seen so many fish and birds in one place before.

After walking for about half an hour you reach the sand spit. The jungle further inland starts to thin out and you can see water through the trees on the other side of the peninsula. Gradually even the palm trees are left behind and the only plants you see are low scrub and tough grasses whose roots cling for dear life onto the sand.

An old weather-beaten sign explains that the sand spit is the nesting place for migratory birds. It asks you to watch where you walk so you don't disturb any nests by mistake.

Not wanting to frighten or harm the nesting birds, you are careful where you step, keeping to the water's edge and away from the dunes. Small grey birds with pale yellow plumage on their chests scurry around, screeching at you whenever you get too close. You admire these mother birds for their bravery in chasing off something so much larger than themselves.

The sand spit is littered with bleached shells that have been washed up over time. In the wet sand you can see bubbles. The bubbles and the old shells lying about make you think there must be quite a few shellfish hiding under the sand. You dig in your toes and sure enough a small scallop is uncovered. You pick up the shell and inspect it. It is a half circle with ridges in the shell radiating out like a child's drawing of the sun. The other side of the shell is the same and you notice a small hinge that holds the two side of the cream and pink shell together.

After looking at the shell for a few moments, you drop it back onto the wet sand and are amazed at how it manages to wriggle its way back under the sand and disappear. Then, with one last bubble, it's gone.

The sun is hot so you pull your floppy hat and sunglasses out of your daypack and put them on. You are pleased you brought water and take a long sip. The sunglasses make it much easier for you to look though the water to the seabed below. You decide to walk with your feet in the shallows to cool off a bit as you continue towards the lighthouse.

A flash of color glints from under the crystal clear water a little way off shore. You stop and stare, trying to see what has caused the sparkle. Little fish dart left and right.

Was it just the light catching the side of a silver fish, or could this be the treasure you are looking for?

You drop your gear and wade in to the water to get a better look at whatever is reflecting the light. By the time you are waist deep, you realize the water is far deeper than you first thought.

Back on the beach you take your snorkeling gear out of

your bag and strip down to your bathing suit and then wade out into the bay. After rinsing out your mask, you fit it to your face, pop in the snorkel's mouthpiece and stick your head under the water to try to see what is glimmering.

Out in deeper water you see a twinkle of sunlight reflecting off something. The glimmer isn't moving so you figure it isn't a fish. You lie on your stomach and paddle out along the surface with your face in the water, breathing through your mouthpiece, until you are directly over what looks like a gold coin resting on the sandy bottom.

You can feel your heart beating in your chest. You can't believe your eyes. Could this be your first discovery?

After taking a deep breath you dive. Down and down you go. The water is so clear everything looks much closer than it actually is. As you dive you kick with all your strength, scooping water with your cupped hands. You are so deep the pressure is starting to hurt your ears.

Just as your hand reaches for the coin, a shadow races along the sandy bottom. The shadow is huge and moving quickly. You snatch the coin off the sand and flip onto your back, looking for whatever it is that is causing the shadow. You hope it isn't a shark.

It only takes a moment to find what you are looking for. Near the surface, a manta ray flies like a bird, its wings barely moving as it glides through the water. The ray's mouth is as wide as the front grill of a car and it wings stretch out and then curve up at their tips. Behind the ray swishes a snake-like tail.

You relax a little. You know that despite being big, manta rays aren't dangerous. You watch entranced as the manta ray passes, but then your lungs start to burn. You push off the bottom and head for the surface, desperate for air, clutching the coin in your hand.

After your head breaks the surface, you spit out your mouthpiece and gulp in air. After a few deep breaths you take off your mask and hook its strap over your wrist and start dog paddling back towards the beach, happy with your discovery.

Sitting in the sand at the edge of the water, you study the coin. It is quite rough and looks handmade, not perfectly round like modern coins. On one side there is a cross made from what look like two capital I's. You're pleased you did an online search for treasure before coming on holiday and remember that this type of cross is called a Crusader's Cross, which signified the union of the Catholic Church and the government of Spain back in the old days.

What's even more exciting is the picture of a Lion and a Castle on the back of the coin. This means you've found a gold Spanish doubloon! The doubloon was a common coin at the time of the Spanish conquistadors. The Spanish exchanged them for trade goods in the New

World for nearly two hundred years.

Have you found part of a pirate's treasure? Or is it a coin washed up from some ancient shipwreck? The coin looks pretty knocked around.

You're keen to go and look for more coins, but just as you put on your snorkel again, you see a triangular grey fin cruising back and forth along the beach. It's hard to tell if the fin is a shark or a dolphin. You wait for a while to see if you can get a better look at what sort of fish the fin belongs to, but whatever it is swims off before you can identify it. You wait a few more minutes to see if it comes back, but it doesn't.

It's time to make a decision. Do you:

Go back into the water and look for more coins? **P13**

Or

Keep walking towards the lighthouse? **P16**

You have decided to go left and head towards the old fortress.

You head down to the firm sand where the walking is easier and start your journey towards the old fortress. It is an imposing looking place even if it is in ruins. Stone walls rise vertically out of the cliffs almost as if they grew there. Only the crude joints in the massive stones used to construct the fortress walls give any hint to them being manmade.

The tower at one end of the fortress is still standing, although its roof has long gone. Along one wall, three ancient cannon point out to sea. These cannon once protected the fort and the village from pirate raiders that used to sail these seas many years ago.

The waves are bigger down this end of the beach. You can see white water spraying high into the air when the waves crash onto the rocks ahead. Further inland, the rugged slopes that lead up the fortress are covered in dense jungle. A layer of mist hangs near the fortress as steam rises from the humid jungle below.

In the ocean, not far from the fortress, is a small island with lush vegetation growing on it. Much of the island's shoreline is steep and rocky, but you notice a small patch of sandy beach at the near end. You can't see any huts on the island, and it looks too small to have fresh water on it, so you doubt anyone lives there.

The sun shines in your eyes as you walk, so you pull a pair of sunglasses out of your daypack and put them on. This makes everything so much easier to see.

Before long, the sandy beach becomes rocky and you are hopping from rock to rock across the tidal pools. You are pleased you wore runners rather than sandals because the surface underfoot is sharp and slippery with spray.

As you work your way around one of the larger pools you look down into its clear water and see tiny fish, starfish, urchins and miniature crabs. The pool is like a little village. The small fish swim in schools around the pool, darting here and there in perfect unison.

You stop for a moment to watch the animals. One little hermit crab has found a discarded shell to use as a home. The shell is much larger than the little crab and he struggles to carry its weight. A fish comes to investigate and the crab disappears into the shell for protection until the fish leaves. You watch as a delicate starfish moves, one tentacle at a time, over the rocks, and see small limpet shells stuck firmly to the rocks, waiting for the tide to come in and refresh the pool. Seaweed necklaces drift on the pool's surface like strings of brown pearls.

After negotiating your way around the tide pools, you find a rocky shelf to walk on. This shelf runs along the bottom of the cliffs and is worn smooth from the action of the waves. In some places where the rock is softer, caves have been eroded into the hillside. You poke your head into one cave, but it only goes back a little way and is dark and damp.

As you near the old fortress, the cliffs get steeper and higher, and the waves breaking on the rocks further out to sea get bigger and wilder. You wonder how safe it is to walk here, and if there are rock falls from time to time. You see quite a few rocks along the shelf, but you're not sure if they've tumbled down from above, or been tossed up by the sea in a storm. The rocks don't have the remains of barnacles or other sea life on them so you suspect they've fallen from high above.

When a fist-sized rock smacks into the ledge twenty yards ahead, your suspicions are confirmed. The shelf is getting narrower and narrower with each step you take. With rocks coming down from above, you realize there is serious danger in going any further.

You are about to turn around when you notice an unusual looking cave. It is unlike all the other caves you've seen. This one has light shining into to it from above somehow. The other caves you've seen are just shallow holes that narrow quickly and go nowhere, but you can see well into this one. The cave interests you, but you are unsure of what to do. Do you investigate further?

As you think, you kick the ground just inside the mouth of the cave with your toe. When you see a glint of light at your feet, you bend down to see what your kicking has uncovered.

It is an old coin. On one side is a cross, on the other a castle and a lion. You've seen these before online and can't believe your luck. You've found a gold doubloon!

Did the pirates drop this coin when they went into the cave to stash their treasure? Was it tossed up by some big storm?

You have a decision to make. Do you:

Go inside the cave to investigate? **P57**

Or

Go back past the rock pools and try to find another way up to the fortress? **P60**

You have decided to go back into the water and look for more coins.

The fish fin hasn't returned for over ten minutes. You wade into the water and put on your face mask and snorkel. As you paddle back out to where you found the coin you scan left and right for sharks. You're scared, but you also want to find more coins.

Floating on the surface, you scan the sea floor below. You scan again for sharks before swimming further away from shore. A little further out you see that coral is growing on something sticking up from the bottom. It looks man-made. Could it be part of a sunken ship?

You kick your feet and head out towards the outcrop. The sandy bottom has given way to rocks and coral. Flower-like anemones sway in the current and tiny fish are everywhere.

There are fish with orange and white stripes, fish of bright blue and others of yellow and red. Schools of bright silver fish race past, zipping one way and then the other, moving together like a troupe of dancers. Some fish weave around the tentacles of the anemones for protection, others pick at the algae growing on the rock.

Occasionally there is a flash of silver as a larger fish swoops in for a meal. The smaller fish scatter quickly in all directions, but once the danger has passed they reform into schools again.

When you reach the outcrop that has caught your attention, you see an old anchor, encrusted with barnacles and other sea life, jammed between two large rocks.

You take a deep breath and dive down towards the anchor. As you swim down, you wonder if the anchor is from an old Spanish galleon or from a more modern vessel. As you reach the anchor, you grab on to its shaft to keep yourself from floating upward as you look around. With so many things growing on the surface of the anchor, you can't tell its age. You can't even tell if the shaft is made of wood or metal. You've decided to have a quick look for coins before your air runs out, when you see a shadow moving across the seabed. This time you can tell it isn't another manta ray, but that of a large shark.

Your air is nearly gone. You have no option but to head for the surface, but before you head up, you grab a rock to use for protection should the shark attack. The rock can't be too big because you won't be able to reach the surface with too much weight, but too small a rock won't be of much use for fighting off a hungry shark.

You grab a medium sized rock and push off the bottom. As you kick up towards the surface you scan the surrounding water for signs of the shark.

But sharks are the ocean's most effective predator. You don't stand a chance. The shark hits you from behind and drags you out into deep water. You try to swing the rock, but everything goes black.

Sorry but this part of your story is over. You made a poor decision and went back into the water after seeing a fin that could have been a shark. Now you've become the shark's lunch.

It is time for you to make another decision. Do you:

Go back to the very beginning of the story? **P1**

Or

Go back to your previous decision and make the other choice? **P16**

You have decided to keep walking towards the lighthouse.

You are pleased that you've decided to keep walking rather than go back into the water. The fin has returned and is cruising just off the beach. You can see now that it was not a dolphin but a big and hungry looking shark. Smaller fish in the shark's path are jumping out of the water in their attempt to get away.

This has brought the birds back and they start dive-bombing the fish.

You tuck the gold doubloon safely away in your pocket and start walking towards the lighthouse, eager to find more treasure.

As the spit curves around, you can see the resort and the local village far across the bay. The houses of the village are small compared to the multi-story buildings of the new resort. It's so different from the houses of your neighborhood.

You can just make out the small fishing boats pulled up onto the sand. Wet fishing nets glisten in the sun as they dry, strung out on poles in the warmth of the sun. They remind you of giant spider webs.

You are so busy looking back at the village as you walk you almost step on a nest. It's only the desperate call of the mother bird that alerts you to it as she screeches and struts back and forth in front of you.

Then you hear a voice call out. "Hey watch it!"

When you turn towards the sound you see a boy about the same age as you carrying a net bag of shellfish. Around the boy's neck is a string of shells. His skin is burnt brown by the sun.

"You've got to watch out for the nests," the boy says shaking his head.

"Sorry," you say as you step carefully around the nest. "I was busy looking at the village and not watching where I was going."

The boy shrugs. "These birds are endangered you know. Didn't you read the sign?"

"Yeah I saw it."

The boy looks at you suspiciously.

Then you explain how you've come out here on the spit to look for pirate treasure, not to harm the birds. "Have you ever found any gold coins out here on the sand spit when you've been digging for shellfish?"

"No," the boy says shaking his head. "But the village elders tell stories about pirates and treasure, stories that their parents told them. I've heard them repeated all my life."

"Could you tell me what you've heard?" you ask the boy.

"I could, but I've got to get these scallops back to the village. My mother will be annoyed if I'm late."

"Yeah I know what you mean. Mine's like that too."

"But if you want to come by the village when you get back from your walk, I can tell you some stories. How does that sound?"

"That would be great," you tell the boy.

"My house is the one nearest the red and blue fishing boat. You shouldn't have any problem finding it."

You thank the boy and he heads off toward the village, turning once to give you a wave.

"Remember to watch out for birds."

You wave back and smile, then carry on toward the lighthouse.

As the sun rises higher in the sky, the heat of the day increases. You take the water bottle out of your pack and drink. The water is lukewarm but at least it's wet.

As you drink, you watch a family of crabs scuttle sideways across the sand. Their eyes are black and stand out bead-like on stems. Their bodies are bright orange and shiny. When you approach for a closer look the crabs turn towards you and lift their pincers into the air for protection. A big one rushes towards you and you leap back.

You imagine the nip those big pincers could give you and stay well clear. One advances on you again and you laugh at his antics as he waves his arms around and snaps his claws.

You walk around the crabs and pick up the pace. Before long you reach the lighthouse.

The lighthouse sits on a base of large rocks concreted together to form a wide flat platform. The platform is taller than you, but a narrow set of steps lead up to the base of the building on one side.

Rusted handrails allow you a handhold on the slippery algae covered steps.

The lighthouse tower is white with bright red stripes running around it. A structure made of glass windows with a peaked roof and a white balcony crown its top. There is a brass plaque mounted on the outside wall near a big steel door.

You climb up the steps to investigate further.

The brass plaque has gone a little green over time, but the engraved words are still quite clear. You step a little closer and read.

Beware of the sea. For under these calm waters lay many shattered dreams.

As you think about the words written on the plaque you walk over to the lighthouse's door. Its surface is bubbled with rust, but it hinges are big and strong and its paint is fresh and white. You turn the handle to see if the door is unlocked, but it does not move.

From the base of the lighthouse you get a great view of the surrounding area. As you look back in the direction from which you've come, you see that the tide is on its way in and the water is coming further and further up the beach with every minute that passes.

You can also see a narrow path, paved with crushed shells on the other side of the sand spit. It looks like it leads back toward the village through the jungle.

So what do you do?

It is time to make a decision. Do you:

Head back to the resort the way you came? **P34**

Or

Follow the shell covered path into the jungle? **P24**

You have decided to head back to the resort along the beach.

You climb down from the lighthouse and walk down to the beach. The tide is coming up so you are forced to walk higher to avoid getting wet. You wonder how much higher the water will come up before you get back to the resort. You can see piles of seaweed and small pieces of driftwood near the high tide mark.

You figure this is as high as the water will come up so you relax and get into your stride. You only have an hour or so before you are expected back at the resort. You don't want to get into trouble because then you might not get to go out on your own to explore any more of the island.

As you walk along the high tide mark you watch the antics of the birds. Most of the time you're alerted by the parent birds whenever you get close to a nest.

When you look down the beach, the resort is a long way away. You didn't realize how far you'd walked, so you speed up a little in the hope of making up some time.

You hear a splash out in the water and turn to see what is going on. Now there are not one, but four sinister grey fins swimming back and forth along the beach. Only little fish are jumping out of the water at first, but then even bigger fish are leaping for their lives. When the seabirds dive in to feast on the sardines stirred up by the sharks, the ocean is turned into a battle ground for survival. Everything that moves is searching for a meal.

Walking so far has made you a little bit weary. You want to stop and take a break, but you also know your family will worry if you are late.

Not much further down the beach, you hear a frantic chirping. In front of you a mother bird is telling you off for getting too close to her nest. As you move inland a little to give the nest a wide berth you notice a small mound of stones. The stack looks like a marker of some sort. It certainly isn't a natural formation.

You walk towards the pile, curious to see what it is.

The cairn is nearly waist high. The stone on top is flat and has a compass rose engraved onto its surface. A needle on the rose points towards the jungle.

You stand behind the cairn and look in the direction of the arrow. It points to a tall tree a couple of hundred paces into the jungle.

The cairn has a bright green lichen growing on the shady sides, indicating to you that it has been there for quite some time. You scrabble around in the sand at the base of the cairn in case something is buried nearby but you find nothing.

You're not quite sure what the arrow indicates, but you hope it could be a clue to finding some treasure.

Is the arrow pointing to the big tree, or something else? You scratch you head as you think. What now?

It's time for you to make a decision. Do you:

Follow the arrow, and head towards the big tree in the jungle? **P31**

Or

Follow the beach back to the resort? **P34**

You have decided to follow the shell covered path.

The shell covered path crunches underfoot as you walk. It is narrow but well maintained. You suspect it leads to the village and resort, but there are so many twists and turns that you're not completely sure. You hear animals moving around in the undergrowth.

Maybe this is a path that is used by the villagers when they go hunting or fishing. But then again, maybe it leads somewhere else altogether.

You know your parents will worry if you are away too long, so even though your legs are tired from walking, you start to jog along the path in an attempt to get back to the resort.

Every few minutes you slow down to a walk and have a bit of a breather. Your water is nearly gone. You hope there are signs of civilization soon. One time when you slow for a rest, you think you hear the sound of moving water in the distance.

Then a few minutes later, you come around a bend in the path and see a small stream heading into a gully. The jungle is denser here because of the water. Huge ferns crowd the stream on both sides.

The stream at this point is barely a trickle. The sand is absorbing the water almost as quickly as it comes down the slope.

You walk upstream for a while in the hopes of finding a

pool deep enough to drink from.

After ten minutes or so you find a shallow pool between some moss-covered rocks. Bright red dragonflies hover over the pool, and funny mosquito-like insects skitter across the water's surface.

The water looks clean but how do you tell? If the stream were near the village you'd never drink out of it for fear of getting sick, but out here in the jungle, chances are it's okay.

You're very thirsty so you fill your bottle and take a little sip to test it. The water tastes wonderful and fresh. You drink your fill and then top up your water bottle. Who knows how long it will be before you find more?

After rejoining the path and walking for another fifteen minutes or so, you finally hear chickens clucking and the sound of children playing. Soon, the first of the village huts appears.

The villager's huts are simple, with four stout poles set into the ground and walls of corrugated iron. The top of the walls are left open to allow the cool breezes to blow through the hut.

Above the walls a thatched roof made of palm leaves keeps off the rain. It's a warm climate, so most daily living is done outdoors. The huts are small and are used mainly for sleeping. You wonder whether the people living there would like things to be a little different though. The resort must seem like a palace to them.

Once you get to the village, you know your way back to the beach. As you pass the red and blue fishing boat you look for the boy you saw on the beach earlier but he is nowhere to be seen.

A woman, who you assume is his mother, is outside stirring a pot set over a small fire. A man wearing sunglasses sits quietly nearby. The smell of spices wafts into your nostrils, and you realize how hungry you are.

Finally the resort comes into view. The gardens around the resort are full of red hibiscus flowers, fuchsia, and palms.

Down one end of the garden, a young woman is giving a demonstration on how to weave cane. Tourists are crowded around her taking pictures.

After a quick look around, you find your family in the cafe by the pool.

You apologize for being late and then tell them about your adventures. You reach into your pocket and feel the gold doubloon. It would be nice to tell the others about your find, but you decide to wait and see if you can find more before surprising them.

The food at the resort is mainly fish caught locally. You order fish, salad and freshly squeezed orange juice. Your stomach gurgles in anticipation.

Your family, and some other tourists they have befriended, have decided to take a bus into the island's main town further up the coast and ask if you want to come along.

You wonder if the town has a library. Maybe you could find some more information about the local history and pirate treasure before you go and see the village boy.

After your family finishes eating, everyone goes to change out of their bathing suits and grab their cameras, wallets and other things they want to take to town.

You transfer the gold doubloon into the pocket of your clean shorts without anyone seeing it, and grab some stationery and a pen from the desk drawer so you can take notes if you find out anything interesting.

The pale green bus is old and battered. There is no glass in the windows. Most of the people on board are locals from the village. One woman has a small metal cage with two chickens squashed inside. One chicken stares at you with its beady eyes as it cluck, cluck, clucks.

The road to town runs past a few huts. Up the hill to your right is the old fort. Then it turns inland and enters the dense jungle.

Under the canopy the road winds through a series of small hills and then drops back down to the coast. This northern part of the island isn't protected by a reef or sand spit so the waves pile in from the open ocean without obstruction.

At one point the bus stops to let off a couple of young men carrying surfboards. Ten minutes later you are bumping along through farm land and then the town finally comes into view.

A concrete breakwater protects the town's small harbor from the fury of the waves. A small coastal trader is moored up to the wooden wharf. A steel crane standing high on rusted metal stilts lifts pallets from the deck of the ship onto a waiting flat-bed truck. A man in a fluro vest stands nearby with a clipboard, counting the goods as they come off the ship.

Just south of the wharf there is a big grassy area where locals have set up market stalls filled with fresh fruit and vegetables, crafts, cages of live chickens and fish of all descriptions.

Rather than look around the market, some tourists decide to check out the museum. You decide to tag along with them and see if you can find a library. Maybe it will have some book on the local history. If not, the museum might have an exhibit about pirates.

Everyone agrees to meet back at the bus stop in two hours.

On the way to the museum, you see a small stone building that looks like a library. You tell the others that you want to do some research and that you'll meet them at the museum or back at the bus stop depending on how long it takes.

After listening to a lecture about being careful and to make sure you are back at the bus stop on time, you set the alarm on your phone as a reminder and then head over and enter the library.

It's not as big as the library at home, and they don't have Wi-Fi so you can't check your email, but you soon locate the local history section and start leafing through the books and forget all about technology.

In one old book you find a picture of the lighthouse and accounts of all the ships lost on the reef before it was built. Historians estimate over twenty ships have gone down in the area. Some were rumored to be laden with gold, silver, and gemstones being transported from Mexico back to Spain.

You find fascinating tales of seamanship and bravery. Some of the wrecks were the result of bad navigation, others by hurricanes that sometimes affect the area. One story you read is of a ship that ran aground on the sand spit while trying to flee pirates. But no matter how hard you look, you can't find any reference to buried treasure.

You jump when your phone beeps. You can't believe that nearly two hours has passed. It's time to rush back to the bus.

Your family is waiting nervously when you come around the corner just as the bus is pulling up.

"Talk about cutting it fine," your mother says, giving the brim of your cap a tweak.

On the ride back to the resort you tell them all you've discovered about shipwrecks and the history of the lighthouse. Before long, the bus is dropping you off outside the resort.

You go up to your room and restock your pack with a couple of chocolate bars and another bottle of water.

You grab a sweatshirt in case it gets cold and take the lighter that is sitting next to the gas stove in the kitchen and then head back to the beach.

You have a decision to make. Do you:

Go and meet the village boy? **P41**

Or

Use one of the resort's small dinghies and go for a sail? **P49**

You have decided to follow the arrow towards the tree in the jungle.

You look up at the big tree and then back at the lighthouse behind you to get your bearings. You know that once you enter the jungle you won't be able to see the tree or the lighthouse from the ground. You need to work out a way to keep walking straight and not end up going around in circles.

You find a smaller tree on the edge of the jungle that is in line with both the lighthouse and the big tree in the jungle and head for that. It is only a few hundred steps across scrub and low, grass covered dunes to the small tree. Once you get to the small tree, you look back across the dunes at the lighthouse and then pick another tree further into the jungle that is in line with the lighthouse and the smaller tree you first used as a landmark. By repeating this procedure you figure you can keep your direction straight enough to find the big tree.

The jungle is cool and shady. When you look up, only small patches of sky can be seen between the outstretched branches of the many trees and shrubs.

A small red headed, yellow breasted hummingbird hovers near a bright pink flower, sucking nectar with its long beak. The broad leafed plant reminds you of the lilies back home only much, much larger.

You stop and listen, amazed by all the unusual sounds.

High in the canopy, you hear a loud squawking. It takes a moment for your eyes to adjust to the low light, but before long you see a toucan with its black and white body, yellow beak and bright blue eyes singing for a mate. Two bright green parrots sit on a branch nearby, plucking at red berries with their strong pink and grey beaks. The parrot's cheeks have a patch of red making it look as though they are blushing.

You would like to stay and watch, but you know that you need to get moving. You also need to focus, otherwise you might become disorientated and lose your way.

After repeating your technique for keeping your course straight a few times you finally come to the big tree. Its root system is like a swarm of giant snakes, twisting and turning as they wind around and then finally go underground. From this unusual root system a large trunk emerges covered in moss and lichen and small delicate ferns.

You raise your head and look up. The tree trunk seems to go on forever. Vines hang from above and colonies of other plants live in the tree's branches. You've never seen so many things growing on a single tree. Then you notice that some of the vines hanging from the tree have been woven into a ladder of sorts. Is this what the arrow on the rock was pointing you towards? Or are you imagining things? Maybe this is just how these particular vines grow?

Through some shrubs to your left you see a pathway covered in white shells that lead off into the jungle in the direction of the village.

You have a decision to make. Do you:

Have a go at climbing the big tree? **P37**

Or

Follow the shell covered path into the jungle? **P24**

You have decided to follow the beach back to the resort.

You decide to head back to the resort rather than go further into the jungle. Not that you are afraid, it's just that you'd like to go sailing out to the island off the other end of the beach.

You turn your back on the cairn of stones and carefully pick your way through the nesting birds back to the beach. Off in the distance, there is a family walking in your direction with two small children carrying buckets and shovels.

The family stops and lays out their beach towels and then puts up a brightly colored umbrella. The elder of the two children wanders down to the wet sand and starts digging, filling up the bucket with sand and then flipping it over to create the walls of a sandcastle.

The smaller child is five or six perhaps. His mother is covering him with sun block. After completing this important task, the mother and father lie on their towels and pull books out of their bag.

The smaller child joins his elder sister. He wants to help build the sandcastle, but it looks like the sister isn't that keen on his help. Maybe his building skills aren't quite up to scratch.

The sister waves her arm and the little boy decides to wander down and paddle in the water instead.

The water is calm enough, but you remember the grey fins you saw earlier and wonder where the sharks have gone. You can't see them at the moment, but you hope the little boy doesn't go any deeper.

You pick up your pace. You want to warn the parents of the sharks you saw earlier and are closing the gap between yourself and them quite quickly when a fin appears not far offshore. And it's heading straight for the young boy who is standing, chest deep in the water slapping the surface with his hands.

The shark must think the boy slapping the water is an injured fish. You shout a warning and start running.

The parents hear you yelling, and look up. They don't understand why you are running down the beach as fast as you can towards their children.

Then the father spots the fin and leaps to his feet. But he is too far away to reach his son in time.

You hit the water at a gallop and plough in, hooking your arm around the waist of the boy and drag him kicking and screaming through the water towards the beach.

The father arrives at your side and scoops up his son. You can see him trembling.

"My god that was close. Thank you so much!"

Your lungs are burning from your exertions. You gasp a quick "That's okay," and suck the warm air into your lungs. You are shaking too.

The young boy is oblivious to the close call he's just had. He's crying, not because of the shark, but at his shock at being dragged so abruptly from the water.

When his father puts him down, he heads straight back towards the water.

The father grabs his arm and tries to explain why he can't go back in the water. In the end the family decides it's probably safer to go back to the resort and the pool.

You wave goodbye, happy to have been the hero and stroll on down the beach past the village and onward to the resort.

It is time for you to make a decision. Do you:

Grab one of the resort's small sailboats? **P49**

Or

Go and meet the village boy? **P41**

Or

Go check in with your family? **P83**

You have decided to have a go at climbing up the tree.

The vines hanging down from the tree are about as thick as your thumb and strong enough to hold your weight when you pull down on them. Many of the vines have twisted around each other in such a way that there are plenty of footholds within reach.

You have always been pretty good at climbing trees but you have never had a go at climbing one so large before. You look up, swallow, then grab a vine and start climbing.

The higher you climb, the more vines you have to hold on to. It is a long way up to the first branch. A couple of times during the climb, you stop to rest your aching legs.

When you finally reach the first branch you sit and look down. Everything below looks a long way away. Parrots squawk and zip past you on their way to the next bunch of berries.

There is a bed of ferns in the crook of the tree that provides you with something soft to lean against. It's like having a recliner chair in the canopy.

You lay back and rest against the fern fronds. As you do so, you stare up into the higher branches. It's amazing how much wildlife there up here.

So far you've counted six different birds, numerous butterflies, moths, flying insects of all sorts and even a small rodent of some sort.

You can see for miles from your vantage point. Then you notice something odd. There is a short piece of brass pipe lashed to one of the bigger branches with old hemp rope. The rope has been varnished to protect it from the elements. Why would anyone would put something like that up in the tree?

Holding onto a branch for support, you stand up and look more closely at the pipe.

Then closing one eye, like you would when looking through a telescope, you peer through one end to see if it is pointing at something in particular.

The only thing you can see through the pipe is the top of the little island that sits offshore from the old fortress.

Is this a clue left by the pirates? Is the island the place you should be exploring if you want to find treasure?

You are lying in the crook of the tree again, thinking about this new development, when you notice one of the branches above you is moving. It is wriggling.

Then you realize it isn't a branch at all, but a large python! The mottled pattern on the snake's back helps it blend in with the foliage so well, you nearly missed it altogether. The bad news is that the snake is heading down the tree towards you far quicker than you like.

The snake is big, maybe not big enough to swallow you whole, but it is certainly big enough to create a serious problem if it wrapped its strong muscular body around you. It could strangle you, or even make you fall out of the tree. You've read that python bites, although not poisonous, can cause serious infection because of the bacteria in their mouths.

You grab onto the vines again, ready to scoot back down, but then the snake turns off onto a higher branch and twists and turns its way out to the end where a nest made of twigs and moss has been built by a bird.

You admire how easily the snake makes it way out to the end of the branch. Then the snake's head disappears over the lip of the bird's nest only to return with an egg in its mouth. The snakes mouth hinges back to allow the egg to slide into its throat before it goes back for another. The lump in the snake's belly is easily visible. A mother bird sits on a branch nearby squawking in distress, helpless to save her babies.

There is a piece of broken branch lodged in the crook of the tree, and you feel sorry for the mother bird. You grab the branch and hurl it up towards the snake as hard as you can. The lump of wood barely clips the snake's tail before falling to the ground, but it is enough to give the snake a fright.

The problem is, now the snake is headed your way, and it's moving fast!

If you sit still, will the snake slither right on by you? Or, in its frightened state, will it give you a nasty bite and potentially ruin your holiday.

Are you in danger of being strangled? Or is it just as

afraid of you are you are of it?

What should you do?

You have a decision to make. Do you:

Sit still and hope the snake passes you by? **P54**

Or

Grab the vine, slither back down the tree and keep following the shell covered path towards the village? **P24**

You have decided to go and meet the village boy.

You are keen to find the village boy you met on the beach and see if you can get more information. The stories that the village elders tell the children might contain clues about where to find more doubloons.

As you enter the village, you are surrounded by curious children, dogs, and even the odd chicken.

You notice many of the dogs look similar. They are mainly tan in color, have short legs and long bodies. Some follow the children on the lookout for scraps of food they might drop, and some lie in the shade with their tongues hanging out.

As you head towards the beach, you keep an eye out for the red and blue boat the boy described. Then you see it pulled up on the sand.

In a hut nearest the boat, a woman who you assume is the boy's mother, is outside stirring a large pot set on a metal stand over a small fire.

A man wearing shorts and sunglasses, probably the boy's father, sits in a chair a few yards away.

You approach the woman and ask her if her son is around. She tells you that he has gone off to collect coconuts. She points towards a group of trees up the beach and you see a small figure up a coconut palm swinging a machete.

"Thank you," you say to the woman and trot off to

speak to the boy.

When you reach the tree the boy has climbed, you watch out for falling coconuts. Five are already on the ground near your feet.

"Hello up there," you yell.

He looks down and smiles. Then he chops down two more coconuts before walking down the tree trunk using only his hands and feet.

When the boy reaches the ground he picks up one of the coconuts and with skilful use of the machete chops off the fibrous outer husk until he gets to the hard shell of the nut itself.

With a quick chop he opens a small hole on one end of the coconut and hands it to you.

"Here, drink," he says.

You take the coconut and bring the hole to your lips and let the sweet milk flow into your mouth. It is the most refreshing thing you have ever tasted.

When you have finished drinking the milk, the boy takes the coconut and cracks it open with the blunt side of his machete. Then he levers a piece of white flesh off the brown shell and hands it to you.

You bite right in and chew the piece up. The boy takes a piece and does the same, all the while smiling with his eyes.

When you've both had your fill, he gathers up the other coconuts and puts them into a mesh bag and slings it over his shoulder. You walk beside him as he heads back to the village.

"Tell me a pirate story," you say.

"Okay. Just let me drop these off first."

"You seem to be working all the time," you say.

The boy gives you a funny look. "Gotta work to eat around here."

You feel your face go red. "Sorry, I didn't mean to…"

"It's alright."

When you get back to the hut, his mother takes the mesh bag. "Okay you two, now get out from under me feet, I've work to do."

"Race you to the water," the boy says before taking off in a sprint.

You fling down your pack and follow as fast as you can.

The boy hits the water and after two long strides arches into a graceful dive and disappears under its glassy surface. You try to do the same, but your dive is more like a belly flop than a proper dive. Still, the water is cool and refreshing after your long walk.

After a quick swim you grab a towel out of your pack and the boy leads you to a patch of shade under a broad-leafed shrub and sits.

"So, you want to hear about pirate treasure do you?"

You nod eagerly. "Yes please."

"Okay," the boy says. "Here is one my grandmother tells about the last shots fired from the fortress."

"The year was 1726. A pirate and his crew of buccaneers were terrorizing the Spanish fleet in the waters of the Caribbean. The pirate was an ex British sailor who had talked the crew of a ship he was serving on at the time to mutiny."

"After taking over the ship, he installed himself as captain and started attacking the Spanish. Within a year he had four ships in his fleet. According to legend, he and his men were responsible for the loss of over twenty Spanish ships and a large amount of Spanish gold."

"Spain, you see, had taken to sending their treasure ships back home in convoys in an attempt to stop the pirates from looting their gold. But the pirates were fearless and sometimes just a little crazy."

You look at the boy and smile. You remember reading about such pirates online, but you weren't sure if the accounts were exaggerated or real.

"You see," the boy continues. "The pirate captain and his crew knew the waters in these parts far better than the Spanish, and they used all sorts of tricks to attack the gold laden ships heading back to Spain."

"One trick was pretending to attack the convoy with a single ship. Then, when the Spanish chased the pirates, the lightly loaded and much quicker pirate ship would escape by running through a narrow channel in a reef unknown to the Spanish. By the time the Spanish saw the danger ahead, it would be too late and their ship would be on the rocks."

"Before the other ships in the convoy could come to the damaged ship's aid, the rest of the pirate fleet would sail out of one of the many hidden coves and attack the floundering ship. Instead of risking further damage, the Spanish convoy would often leave the damaged ship to fend for itself and sail off."

"When given a choice of death or surrender, the crew of the floundering ship would sometimes murder the officers and join the pirates rather than be blown to pieces on the reef."

"Using the crew of the damaged ship as labor, the pirates would strip as many guns and gold off the Spanish ship before it sank. Then they sailed off to one of their hiding spots."

"One of these hiding spots was in the lee of the small island just offshore from where the old fortress sits now. It was a good anchorage protected from the fierce winds that blow around here at certain times of the year."

"But it didn't take long for the Spanish to get angry with the pirates stealing their gold. Using slave labor from the village, they built the fortress up on the cliffs. Once Spanish guns overlooked the calm waters between the little island and the shore, they could anchor in the bay without fear of attack from the pirate raiders."

"But the pirate captain had other ideas. He hated the Spanish almost as much as he loved gold. On a moonless night in the summer of 1726, he and his four ships sailed silently to the seaward side of the small island, hidden from the fortress. One crewman rowed a boat to shore and climbed to the top of the island where the pirates had secretly built a lookout tower. There, he acted as a spotter for the pirate gunners hidden from sight of the Spanish, and directed their fire towards the fort and the Spanish ship anchored in the bay."

"The pirate ships sat broadside to the fortress and aimed their cannon over the top of the island. When all four ships were ready, they fired the first volley before the Spanish even knew they were there."

"The pirate spotter on top of the island signaled the Spanish whereabouts to the gunners on board the ships and the pirates fired again. There were many casualties among the Spanish ships and at the fortress before the Spanish even figured out where the cannon fire was coming from."

"Another group of pirates had landed on the far side of the peninsula, and made their way through the jungle and up the hill under cover of darkness and were waiting to rush the fortress as soon the cannon fire from the pirate ships breached its walls."

"Meanwhile, the onshore wind didn't give the Spanish ships any chance to maneuvers. Most were burning before they even got their anchors up. One of the Spanish ships ran aground on the little island in its attempt to get away.

The wreckage can still be seen on the rocks."

"The next day, the villagers praised the pirates for defeating the Spanish. You see, the Spanish had been stealing the villager's food and mistreating them. The pirate captain was treated like hero. It's even told he married the village chief's daughter."

"So what happened to all the Spanish gold?" you ask the boy.

"There are rumors that the pirates hid some of it around here somewhere, but apart from the odd coin that washes up, very little has ever been found."

"What about on the island?" you ask. "Do you think the treasure could be there?"

The boy shrugs his shoulder. "Could be anywhere I suppose. People have been looking for it for over a hundred years."

You are not encouraged by this information. Still, at least if there is a treasure, it is still out there somewhere.

The boy gets up. "I'd better get home. Mother will have more chores for me."

"Well thanks for the story," you say. "Maybe we can go searching for treasure together some time."

"Sure," the boy says. "Finding some gold would be great. I could pay to get my father's eyes fixed. Once his cataracts are removed he'll be able to go out fishing again."

You wave goodbye and think about what the boy said

about his father. You hope you find some treasure, so you can share some with him.

As you walk down the beach towards the resort you have a decision to make.

What do you do?

Do you:

Go out on one of the resort's small sailing boats? **P49**

Or

Go check in with your family? **P83**

You have decided to take out one of the resort's small sailing boats.

You are keen to get out to the small island. You figure it is an ideal place to find pirate treasure. Sailing is something you've enjoyed for quite a few years. Your local sea scouts group has regular lessons for cadets your age. You're not the best sailor in your corps but you are quite handy around small boats as long as the wind isn't blowing too hard.

A staff member from the resort gives you a lifejacket and a quick run-down on how to operate the boat's sail and tiller. The dinghy has a reasonably short mast and single sail, similar to the ones you've handled before. Rather than having a keel like bigger boats, the dinghy has a centerboard that you drop down through a slot in the bottom of the boat. This acts like a keel and helps keep the boat running in a straight line when you are sailing.

You place your pack into the waterproof compartment under the seat with the flares, spare rope and tiny anchor, push the boat out into the shallows and climb aboard.

After dropping the centerboard and raising the sail you settle down and turn the boat so the wind fills the sail. Instantly the breeze pushes you along through the water.

You keep close to the shore at first to get used to the boat's handling before heading out further into the bay. You find the dinghy reasonably stable and easy to sail.

The wind is light and the waves are small. As long as you remember to duck when the boom swings around when tacking or jibing, it's pretty hard to make a mistake.

After a couple of trial runs back and forth along the beach, you point the boat towards the little island off the coast from the fortress. The onshore wind is the perfect angle for you to make it without having to do too much tacking.

As you sail, the boat tilts with the wind and you hear the water rushing along the hull.

A cheeky seagull comes to investigate the boat. He lands and then sits looking at you with his beady orange and black eyes from the stern of the boat. You can smell the bird's fish-breath from your position by the tiller, but it's nice to have some crew along for the ride.

"Ahoy ahoy," you say to the gull. "Now don't be pooping on the poop deck me hearty."

The seagull turns its head sideways and gives you a look as if to say, 'aye aye skipper' and then swivels its tail feathers over the side and drops a big white splat into the water. A moment later it squawks once and takes off to rejoin the other gulls fishing out towards the sand spit.

As you near the island, you get a good look at the fortress from the water. The cannon barrels pointing in your direction make you nervous, even though you know they are old and rusty. You can imagine how vulnerable those approaching the fortress from the sea must have felt many years ago.

Your sailing instructor taught you to check things out before landing your boat on an unknown beach in case there are hidden rocks that aren't obvious at first. The island isn't that big, so after making a quick pass of the beach, you decide to sail all the way around before landing on the tiny strip of sand.

The water is crystal clear. Even though it is quite deep, you can still see the bottom. The reef around the island is full of colorful fish.

You tack and turn to starboard ready to sail counter-clockwise around the island. When you reach the southernmost end of the island you tack back.

It's amazing how different the island is on the seaward side. It is steep and rocky, with vertical cliffs. They aren't as big as the cliffs on the mainland, but they still tower over the mast of your little boat.

Nesting in holes and cracks in the cliff are thousands of seabirds. As you sail closer the noise from the birds becomes louder and louder. Some of the bolder birds dive bomb your boat in an attempt to scare you away.

Further around past the cliffs, you see the wreckage of a ship on the rocky shore. The wreck looks like it has been there a long time.

Before you know it, you are back where you started having completed your circumnavigation of the island. You line up for your run onto the sandy strip of beach.

Landing will be tricky. You will need to pull the centerboard up out of its slot so it doesn't dig into the sand, and drop the sail at just the right time. Drop the sail too early and you won't have enough speed to reach the beach. Too late and you'll hit the beach hard and risk damaging yourself or the boat.

You are pleased you've done similar maneuvers a few times at home. After judging the speed of the boat and the depth of the water you get ready to lift the centerboard and tuck the halyard holding up the sail under you leg for quick access.

"Three, two, one," you count down.

Just as the water shallows, you pull up the centre board and drop the sail. The boat's momentum carries it onto the beach and the bow eases gently into the soft white sand.

You hop over the side into knee deep water and grab one side of the boat. With your feet digging into the sand, you drag the dinghy as far as you can up the beach to keep it from floating away. Then you take the bowline and loop the rope twice around a sturdy palm tree on the edge of the jungle before tying it off.

Happy the landing has gone so well, you put your hands on your hips and survey your surroundings.

The beach is small, only twenty paces wide. Lush green foliage grows right down to its edge. One end of the beach leads onto the rocks that go about half way around the island towards the shipwreck.

At the other end of the beach, the steep cliffs begin. Inland there are two hills of similar height, with a gully running up between them to the top of the island. You are keen to explore the island further and wonder which way you should go.

It is time for you to make a decision. Do you:

Walk around the rocks to where you saw the remains of a shipwreck? **P85**

Or

Go inland and explore the island? **P88**

You have decided to sit still and hope the snake passes you by.

The snake is moving quickly down the tree. You press your back into the bed of ferns and freeze, hoping it won't notice you.

The snake twists and turns along the branch until it is directly overhead. You want to turn your face up so you can see what it is doing, but you don't want to move and give yourself away.

The snake's scales feel incredibly smooth and cool as they slide over your shoulder and brush your neck. Is the snake about to coil itself around your windpipe and strangle you? Then you see its head moving further down and you feel the weight of the snake's body pressing on your legs.

The tail gives your neck a final flick as it passes and the snake disappears from view further down the tree. A drop of sweat runs down your cheek.

That was a little too close for comfort. Still, it was worth climbing the tree for the clue you've gained about needing to go to the island. Or is this just some game the locals play on the tourists to keep them coming back?

In either case, you want to find out. You grab the vines and start your descent, but find that locating the footholds are much harder when climbing down. You wrap a vine around one ankle and search desperately with your other foot until you locate a place to stand. After resting your arms, you lower yourself down again and repeat the process.

Your hands and arms are tired from holding your weight and your hands are getting slippery with sweat. When you start to slip you manage to hook your arm through a loop to stop yourself from falling. Climbing down isn't as easy as you thought it would be.

Still you have no choice but to continue. You dry one hand at a time on your shirt then start your descent once more. But before long you are sliding down faster than you want. Your hands are burning from the friction. Luckily you are almost down when you let go and fall into the soft undergrowth. You roll as your feet hit the ground but still the wind is knocked out of you.

You lie on the ground and catch your breath. Two close calls in a row have given you the shakes. Surely your luck is due for a change.

After resting a minute you decide to head back towards the resort. You'd like to see if you can get out to the island and see if there is treasure hidden out there.

You also wonder if the boy from the village might have some useful information.

You go to the shell covered path and start walking. After walking for half an hour you come to a small stream and refill your water bottle. At little further on you finally you hear sound of chickens clucking and of the village children playing.

So what now?

It is time for you to make a decision to make. Do you:

Go and meet the village boy? **P41**

Or

Go check in with your family? **P83**

You have decided to go inside the cave to investigate.

The cave's entrance is narrow but a faint light is coming from a crack high up in its ceiling. From somewhere deep in the cave's interior you hear a steady drip, drip, drip of water. The floor of the cave is damp and smooth and you are careful to watch where you step.

You wish you'd brought a flashlight with you, but thankfully there is just enough light from above to see where you are going.

The cave is narrow but the roof above is high. So high in fact, most of the ceiling is shrouded in darkness despite the narrow rays coming from above.

Enormously long stalactites hang from the cave's ceiling. Their paleness in the faint light make them look like icicles ready to drop down and spear anyone underneath them. As you get deeper in the cave, sharply pointed stalagmites grow up from the floor. Eventually the cave narrows and you come up against an almost sheer wall.

You can't go any further.

Before you walk back outside, you run your hand over one of the stalagmites and feel how cool and incredibly smooth it is. Tiny amounts of calcium from the surrounding limestone, dissolved in water and seeping though the ground from above, must have dripped inside this cave for thousands of years, gradually building up layer upon layer for these formations to occur.

You are so impressed you take your camera out of your pack to take a picture. It's pretty dark, but you're confident the flash will provide enough light to get a good shot.

For a brief second, as the camera's flash goes off, more of the interior of the cave comes into view.

It takes a few moments for your eyes to readjust again after the flash, but during that time you wonder if what you saw set into the cave's wall was real or just a trick of the light. You close your eyes and wait for your pupils to dilate again so you can see.

Carefully you walk toward the far wall of the cave with your arms extended. When you reach the smooth stone, you feel around for the narrow flight of steps you saw cut into the sheer rock face.

The steps are smooth and very narrow. There is less light in this part of the cave so your exploration is as much by feel as it is by sight.

The first ten or so steps you can feel with your hands, they are only as wide as your foot and there is no handrail for safety.

You put your back against the wall and take the first few steps sideways, keeping your back hard against the stone. Progress is slow. After half a dozen steps you wonder if this is a good idea. Still, it is lighter higher up towards the top of the caves.

Does this staircase lead all the way up to the fortress? Is it safe to climb?

You have a decision to make. Do you:

Keep climbing the stone steps? **P65**

Or

Go back and try to find another way up to the fortress? **P60**

You have decided to find another way up to the fortress.

Once out of the cave, you notice the tide is coming in and the waves are coming closer and closer to the rocky ledge you've been walking along. Spray is being whipped up by the onshore wind, making the rocks slippery.

Not wanting to hang around on the exposed ledge any longer than necessary, you hurriedly make your way back towards the tide pools.

In the distance you see that the outer pools are already being swamped by the incoming tide.

Once off the ledge, you keep as far from the water as possible as you hop from rock to rock.

When you are nearly back to the beach, you see a pile of stones you hadn't noticed before, standing about as high as your waist on the edge of the jungle. The stones look to be a marker of some sort.

As you walk closer, you see the cairn is capped with a flat stone that has a compass rose and arrow engraved upon it. The arrow is pointing into the jungle. Is this marking an alternative route up to the fortress?

Pulling the branches aside, you make your way in the direction of the arrow. After about twenty steps you come across a path covered in white shells.

The path is narrow and rutted. The jungle closes in on it from both sides. At one time it would have been wide enough for a horse and cart, or even a team of oxen to get up, but now the path is being reclaimed by the jungle and waist high weeds grow amongst the shells. At one point the path cuts across a narrow watercourse flowing directly down the side of the hill. The rocks in the watercourse are covered in a pale white mineral that looks similar to the surrounding limestone cliffs.

It is shady under the dense canopy of branches. You can imagine that travelling the path at night would be difficult. Even with a full moon shining, you can tell that little light would make its way through the trees above.

You figure the shells were most likely put here to help guide the way in the dark, in much the same way that people paint the leading edges of concrete steps so they can see where to go at night.

The pathway is steep and follows the natural contours of the land as much as possible as it zigzags up the hillside. In some places large rocks have been used to bridge gullies or provide extra support for the path along the edge of the hill.

Eventually you arrive at a gate on the inland side of the fortress. Charred timbers are the only remnant of what would have been a solid barrier in its time.

You walk cautiously into the fortress. Most of the walls are still intact, but the central courtyard is a messy jumble of twisted timber and other wreckage.

The fortress shows sign of a battle that must have taken

place here many years ago. In some parts, sections of wall have been destroyed and blackened beams from buildings lay on the ground.

Weeds grow between the flagstones. Along the front wall a set of stone steps lead up to a broad promenade along its top.

Three cannon sit along the top of the wall pointing out to sea. Each cannon sits on a cradle with wooden wheels sheathed in metal of some sort. The cradles are not in good order. One leans awkwardly to one side, a wheel collapsed.

You make your way across the courtyard and up the steps. The top of the wall is broad and paved with flat stones. There is a smaller defensive wall on its outward side to stop people, and the guns, from falling down to the rocks below. When you lean out and look down, you can see the ledge you walked along. From this vantage point it looks like a narrow ribbon of stone pressed hard against the cliff, barely a track at all.

The view from the wall is spectacular. Far off to your right you can see the bay, surrounded by the curve of the sand spit.

The lighthouse looks like a toy in the distance. The resort and the village also look tiny. You can just make out the aquamarine water of the resort's biggest swimming pool. People on the beach look like insects scurrying around.

As you walk along the top of the wall, you look along the barrel of each cannon, trying to gauge what they'd been aiming at the last time they were fired.

Curiously, every cannon is pointing towards the small island off shore. Why would they be shooting at the island? If the fortress was under attack from pirates surely they would want to shoot at the pirate ships, not some speck of land?

You scratch your head as you think. The fortress is silent. All you can hear are the waves crashing below and the chatter of birds from the surrounding jungle. It looks as though nobody has been here for a long time.

As you walk along the wall towards the turret, you come to a statue. The statue is of a man with his arms outstretched as if he is preaching to people gathered in the courtyard below. His body almost forms a cross. In his hand is a book. The statue sits on a high plinth with steps leading up to it.

A small plaque embedded in the plinth says 'embrace the saint'. Are the steps there so you can climb up and hug the statue?

It seems a bit foolish, but you are willing to do anything that helps in your quest. At least no one is around to see you.

So, after ascending the steps, you move into the statue's arms, as if to hug a parent. The statue's tunic is draped in such a way that it creates a groove in the stone for you to rest your chin along as you wrap your arms around the saint's torso. You close your eyes and feel the cool marble press against your chest.

When you open your eyes, your gaze is directed toward the little island offshore. Is that where the treasure is? Is this a clue to where the treasure has been hidden? Is the pirate treasure buried on the island?

It is time to make a decision. Do you

Go back to the resort and find a sailboat? **P49**

Or

Look around the fortress a little more? **P80**

You have decided to keep climbing the stone steps.

With your back hard against the stone wall, you slowly take one step after another. It is quite scary climbing in near darkness. You know that one slip will mean certain injury, if not death. Who would come to your rescue if you were to fall? A slight tremor makes your knees shake. Still you keep climbing.

You are pleased you can't see the floor of the cave below. It must be quite a long way down by now.

As you climb higher, the light from the crack in the cave roof gets a little brighter. You can see holes drilled into the wall further up the staircase. One of these holes has the remnants of a wooden torch stuck into it. You reach up and touch the torch as you pass, but the wood turns to dust in your hand. It makes you wonder how long it has been since someone has been up here.

When you reach the end of the stone steps, you are still quite some distance from the top of the cave. At least the light is much better here. The steps finish on a reasonably wide ledge. You look up.

The crack in the roof of the cave is wider than you first thought, about as wide as a bus and almost as long. It drips with creepers and vines. Some of the vines reach all the way down to the ledge. You go over to investigate.

The vines are about as thick as your thumb and twist around each other creating a natural ladder of sorts. You wonder if the vines will hold your weight and give them a strong tug. They seem pretty strong, so you jam your foot at the junction of two vines and step up. You bounce up and down to test their strength. They feel springy, but solid.

As you look up you see hundreds of butterflies hovering in a huge swarm near the cave's opening. They are beautiful. Their wings are framed in a reddish brown, but the main wing area is nearly clear, creating a stained glass window effect. They fly in circles that form a miniature butterfly tornado in the opening.

When you look along on the ledge again, you notice a couple of the butterflies have fallen and lay dead on the ledge. You pick one up and hold it up to the light. It is so delicate with two long thin antennae and a thin tongue, or proboscis, which curls back on itself and almost makes a complete circle. You take two of the beautiful creatures and put them in the front pocket or your pack, careful to fold the wings neatly against their bodies to keep them from getting damaged.

You legs are sore from the big climb up the steps, so you sit on the ledge and lean against the wall for a breather.

You are thinking about climbing the vine when you see something engraved into the smooth stone wall. You get up to investigate.

The writing is in an old script but once you stand in a

way that allows the maximum of sunlight to shine on it, you can read it.

Climb to the sky and embrace the Saint. Only then will you see your golden future.

You wonder what the inscription means by golden future. And how does one embrace the Saint?

You have a decision to make. Do you:

Climb the hanging vines to the top of the cave? **P68**

Or

Go back down and try to find another way up to the fortress? **P60**

You have decided to climb the hanging vines to the top of the cave.

Once again you place your foot at the junction of where two vines twist around each other and create a place for your foot. It's tricky to see each step because the vines are covered in glossy green heart-shaped leaves, but you find if you hold on with one hand you can pluck the leaves around each foothold as you go up.

After the first few steps you start to get the hang of vine climbing and make your way steadily up towards the roof of the cave. About halfway through the climb you reach the level of the butterflies. They are even prettier up close, with thin dividers between the sections that make up each of the wing panels.

It's a perfect spot for a breather. One of the butterflies lands on your forearm, giving you a closer look. It has six black legs and a narrow body. Its proboscis flicks in and out. When you are ready to start climbing again, you blow gently on the butterfly encouraging it to take off. With a flap of its transparent wings, it joins the others dancing in the sunlight.

Gradually you make your way up the top of the cave and pull yourself over the edge. The climb has taken a lot of energy and it takes a minute to catch your breath.

You sit up and look around. Lush foliage stretches in all directions and you wonder how many people have fallen down this hole by mistake. The jungle around the hole is foreign to you. Dense vegetation of every description crowds in. It makes you feel like you are the first person to stand here, but then you remember the steps painstakingly cut into the solid rock and laugh at your foolishness. Of course others have been here. Maybe this is where the pirates came to hide their treasure.

The jungle is so thick you have no idea which direction to head. You hope you can find a path somewhere. You walk around the hole, making sure not to trip and fall over the edge as you look for a path.

Then you see a flat stone with an arrow engraved in it wedged into the crook of a gnarled old tree. It points directly uphill along a very narrow and rocky watercourse.

You head up the watercourse thinking that if it leads nowhere at least you'll be able to find your way back to the hole and climb back down to the beach to get back to the resort.

The rocks in the stream have been rounded by the water running over them for so many years. Some of them are creamy white, and look to be coated in the same calcium material that the stalagmites were made of.

Finally after quite a steep climb, you reach the walls of the fortress. Rough blocks of stone tower high about you. There is no way to climb up here, so you turn inland hoping to find a gateway or a section of wall that has been breached so you can get into the fortress.

It is tough going. The jungle is growing right up to the old wall and often you need to work your way past a tangle of branches to keep moving. One tangle of branches is covered in thorns and red flowers making it difficult to pass, but then once you get through you see a section of wall that has partially fallen.

You scale the pile of tumbled down rocks and enter the deserted fortress. Many of the walls are still intact, but the central courtyard is a messy jumble of twisted timber and other wreckage. The fortress shows signs of the battle that must have taken place here many years ago. Parts of the wall have been destroyed and piles of charred beams lay on the ground. Tall weeds grow between the flagstones and a set of stone steps lead up to a broad promenade around the top of the wall. Three cannon sit on the promenade pointing out to sea. Each cannon sits on a carriage of timber that has wooden wheels sheathed in metal of some sort. The carriages are not in good order. One leans awkwardly to one side, its wheel collapsed.

You make your way across the courtyard and up the stone steps to the top of the wall. The top of the wall is broad. There is a smaller defensive wall on its outward side to stop people and the guns from falling down to the rocks below. When you lean out and look down, you can see the narrow ledge you walked along to get to the cave far below.

The view from the wall is spectacular. Far off to your

right you can see the bay, surrounded by the curve of the sand spit. The lighthouse looks like a toy in the distance. The resort and the village also look tiny. You can just make out the aquamarine water of the resort's biggest swimming pool. People on the beach look like beetles scurrying around.

As you walk along the top of the wall, you look along the barrel of each cannon, trying to gauge what they'd been aiming at the last time they were fired.

Curiously, each cannon is pointing towards the small island off shore. Why would they be shooting at the island? If the fortress was under attack, surely they would want to shoot at the pirate ships?

The fortress is silent. All you can hear are the waves crashing below and the chatter of birds from the surrounding jungle. It looks as though nobody has been here for a long time.

You come to a statue just beside the turret on one end. The statue is of a man, his arms outstretched as if he is preaching to people gathered in the courtyard. In his hand is a book. It is an odd pose. The statue sits on a plinth, but steps lead up to it. You remember the message in the cave. It said, embrace the Saint.

You ascend the stairs and step into the statues outstretched arms. The statue's tunic is draped in such a way that it creates a groove for you to rest your chin in as you wrap your arms around the Saint's torso. You close your eyes and relax in the statue's cool embrace. Then you open your eyes and see the island offshore. Is that where the treasure is? Is the statue a clue to finding it? Could gold on the island be what 'a golden future' means?

It is time to make a decision. Do you:

Go back to the hole at the top of the cave and climb back down to the beach and go back to the resort the way you came? **P73**

Or

Leave the fortress and try to find another way back to the resort? **P75**

You have decided to go back to the hole at the top of the cave.

You see a broken and charred gate on the far side of the fortress, but decide to go back over the collapsed wall the way you came in just to be sure you don't miss the track back down the hillside.

Going down is harder than climbing up because you can't reach forward and grab on to things so easily. A couple of times you slip on the smooth rocks as you descend. You slow down as you get close to the top of the hole, not wanting to slip over the edge.

The hole appears below you as a gaping crack in the earth. You work your way around the side and look for the vines that you climbed up. It's hard to tell which vines are which from this angle. You regret not marking the right ones.

When you're pretty sure you've found the place to descend, you lie on your belly clutching the vines and lower yourself feet first over the ledge.

It is hot and your hands are sweaty. You twist your head around searching for a foothold. You finally jam your foot over a twist in two vines and are able to take the pressure off your arms.

This isn't as easy as you thought it would be.

Finding the next foothold is just as hard. You arms strain as you try to find a place to rest your foot. This is so much harder than climbing up, when you could easily see where to put your foot as you climbed.

Your arms are aching as you look for a step. Your feet are flailing around desperately. You feel your hands slipping on the vines as your strength starts to go. You try to grip harder, but you can't. You are slipping! The friction burns your hands. The pain is too much and you fall through the darkness.

Unfortunately, this part of your story is now over. You made an unwise decision in trying to climb down the vine. Remember it's often harder climbing down than climbing up, especially when you can't see where to put your feet. Pity you didn't think of that.

But not to worry, you can start over.

It is time for you to make a decision. Do you:

Go back to the very beginning of the story? **P1**

Or

Go back to your previous decision and decide to leave the fortress and try to find another way back to the resort. **P75**

You have decided to try to find another way back to the resort.

The most obvious way to leave the fortress is through a charred gate on the far side of the courtyard.

You step over the massive burnt timbers lying on the ground and step outside the compound where there is an overgrown pathway covered with white shells twisting down the hillside.

After the first sharp corner, the pathway disappears under the canopy into the jungle.

Being unused like it is, the jungle has taken back much of the path. Deep ruts have been cut across it during the rains and the footing is tricky in places.

As you are jumping over one such channel cut into the pathway you notice a huge centipede crawling down its centre.

You can't believe the size of it. You remember reading about the giant centipedes that live here in the Caribbean, but you never dreamed you'd see one!

It is longer than your foot. You stop for a quick look, and then remember that it is also extremely poisonous and feeds on birds, lizards, tarantula spiders, and even bats! Then you remember it is also supposed to be very fast on its many, many feet.

You move down the hill, looking back once or twice to make sure the nasty looking beast isn't following you. This is not an insect you want to mess around with.

About half way down the hill, near the edge of the path, you see a huge spider's web strung between two trees. You move a little closer to have a look. The spider is bright yellow with black stripes on its legs.

You've read about this spider too. It's a banana spider, also known as the Brazilian wandering spider, one of the most lethal in the world! Suddenly the jungle feels like a dangerous place.

Your walk becomes more of a trot as you scrunch down the shelled path. You look right and left, wondering what other lethal creatures are lurking in the jungle ready to leap out and ruin your holiday.

At the bottom of the path you pass a stone cairn. On top of the cairn is a flat stone with a compass rose and an arrow engraved into it pointing back up the hill in the direction from which you've come. You are relieved to be back on the beach.

You pull your water bottle out and drain the last of it into your parched mouth. You try to forget about spiders and centipedes and think about more pleasant things like gold doubloons and pirate treasure. You wipe your mouth with the back of your hand and put your water bottle back in your pack.

There are a few boats out in the bay, but none are sailing near the island. After another half an hour's walk you are back at the resort.

It is time to make a decision. Do you:

Go check in with your family? **P83**

Or

Go and take one of the sailboats out to the island? **P49**

You have decided to go deeper into the underground chamber.

There is very little light as you head down the next flight of steps into the underground chamber. Your hand touches the cool stone of the wall as you descend step by step; more feeling your way than seeing. Dark is closing in on you and the walls are damp with moisture.

It smells musty down here, like dirt and pee and dead animals.

When you reach the bottom of the staircase, you can barely see your hand in front of your face. The ground under your feet is slippery and sloping steeply off into the darkness.

You are beginning to think this was a bad idea when you hear screeching above your head and you realize that what you smell are bats.

And if bats are hanging on the ceiling, it means the slipperiness under your feet is most likely bat droppings.

You turn to go back up, but in the process you slip onto one knee. You don't want to put your hand down in the bat poo so you try to get up without using your hands.

As you lurch to your feet you lose your balance and twist around, both feet slip out from under you and you fall backwards. You reach out to steady yourself, but there is nothing to hold on to. Your shoulder hits the ground with a thud and you find yourself sliding further down the slope.

The further you slide, the steeper the floor becomes, until it is so steep you couldn't get to your feet even if you wanted too. After sliding for ages, you smack hard into a stone wall at the bottom of the ramp.

You are wet, bruised and covered in muck. A faint light shines back at the top of the slope but the slime covered ramp is impossible for you to climb no matter how hard you try. You are stuck in the bowels of the fortress. With luck someone will find you before you die of thirst.

Unfortunately, this part of your story is over. You made a bad decision to go deeper when you didn't have enough light to see properly. Hidden dangers lurked in the darkness.

Luckily you can have another go at getting it right.

It is time to make a decision. Do you:

Go back to the very beginning of the story? **P1**

Or

Make that last choice differently? **P80**

You have decided to look around the fortress a little more.

You turn your back on the statue and walk back along the top of the wall towards the steps leading down into the courtyard. There are a couple of inner doors built into the fortress walls you want to investigate.

Bolted to the wall beside one door is an iron basket filled with the remnants of a fire. The burned wood doesn't look as old as the other charred remains scattered around the courtyard. It makes you wonder if someone else has been up here recently.

The doorway is a wide arch of stones fitted perfectly into the wall without the need for mortar. Two large hinges are set into the wall, but you can't see a door anywhere. You take a step into the passage and turn right. The passage leads to some steps that take you down below ground level.

By the time you are halfway down the steps, the light is fading fast. Then you see a faint light in front of you as you carefully feel you way down the remainder of the steps. A narrow slit in the seaward wall provides you with just enough light to see that you are in a hollowed out chamber below the courtyard, held up with massive stone columns. More iron baskets are attached to the walls, along with a series of iron rings linked together with rusted chain. You shiver when you realize this must have been where the Spanish held their captives.

You poke your head into another doorway and see another flight of steps leading even deeper into the fortress. How many levels are there?

Leaning on its side against one wall is an iron gate. The gate has bars running from top to bottom. On the end of each bar is a sharp spike. This must be the gate from the doorway above, but why has it been taken off its hinges and dragged downstairs?

Then you see that there is a narrow ledge in the wall above the gate. Light from a narrow slit in the ledge is pouring into the underground chamber. Whoever leaned the gate against the wall must have used it as a ladder to climb up to the ledge, but why?

You cross the chamber and test the bars on the old gate. They are rusty, but will still support your weight. Carefully you climb the eight or so bars up to the ledge.

What you see nearly makes you fall, because lying on the ledge is a skeleton.

You scurry back down and try to control your shaking. An image of the skeleton flashes in your mind. There is something not quite right about this picture. Once you stop shaking, you grab onto to the gate and start climbing once more.

As you peer over the edge of the ledge, the skeleton comes back into view. Its bones are white and perfectly laid out, as if a person had climbed up onto the ledge, laid down on their back, and gone to sleep. But that couldn't be what happened. Where are the skeleton's clothes? If the person had died down in this chamber, surely they would have had on rags at least. But there is no sign of any clothing.

Could this skeleton be someone trying to scare other treasure hunters off?

You look out of the narrow window inset into the wall above the ledge. The wall on this part of the fortress is very thick and the window gets smaller and smaller as it goes through the stone. By the time it gets to the opening on the outside of the wall, the opening is only the width of your hand, far too small for a person to fit through.

But it is the view out the window that interests you most. Surely this can't be by chance.

Framed perfectly by the window, across the narrow stretch of water, is the small island.

It is time for you to make a decision. Do you:

Head back to the resort, get a boat and sail out to the island? **P49**

Or

Go down the steps deeper into the underground chamber? **P78**

You have decided to go check in with your family.

Your family are pleased to see you. They yell for you to jump into the pool and join them, so you strip down to your swimsuit and dive in. The water is cool and refreshing after your long walk. You lie on your back and float as your sore muscles relax.

As you float, you watch the birds flit around the flowering shrubs planted around the pool area. They are a noisy lot, and not at all scared by the people. Some birds pick at crumbs dropped on the ground in the outdoor eating area.

For a few minutes you dive and swim and splash the others, but before long you get restless. What you really want to do is go exploring again.

After telling your family that you'll buy them each something special if you find treasure, they seem eager for you to go off again. "Don't come back until you've found something," they say.

You go up to your room for some more supplies. A couple of chocolate bars and a bottle of water from the mini bar should do the trick.

Then you grab a sweatshirt in case it is cold later on as the sun goes down and put that in your pack too. You spot a lighter next to the gas stove in the kitchen and slip it into your pocket, thinking it might come in handy.

After zipping up your pack, you head down the steps to

the reception area, walk through the lobby and head out the front door towards the beach.

It is time to make a decision: Do you:

Go and take one of the resort's sailboats out to the island. **P49**

Or

Go left towards the old fortress? **P9**

Or

Go right towards the lighthouse? **P3**

You have decided to walk around the rocks towards the shipwreck.

You take your pack from the watertight compartment in the sailing dinghy and slip it over your shoulders. The plan is to walk around the rocks to the shipwreck you saw when sailing around the island. There could be all sorts of interesting things to find.

The tide is on its way out. As the minutes pass, more and more rocks are exposed. Hundreds of black mussel shells are attached to those recently exposed, a feast just there for the taking. Maybe you'll gather some of the shellfish on your way back to the beach and steam them open over a small fire.

Getting around the rocks isn't quite as easy as it looked like it would be when you sailed past in the dinghy. In a number of places, deep channels, too wide to jump, run from the ocean right up to the rocky shore making it tricky and a little dangerous. Luckily the waves are small and you are able to negotiate your way by hugging the cliff and using vines hanging from above as handholds as you work your way around towards the wreck.

When the ship comes into view, you are amazed how big it is. Huge ribs curve up and out from the massive timber keel. Few of the hull planks remain, most having been washed away over years by the many storms that frequent these parts.

Below the bowsprit, attached to the solid prow of the boat, is the wooden figure of a woman. Her back is attached to the ship, her chin is up, chest thrust forward, arms calmly down by her sides. She looks as if she is surrendering herself to the sea, passive yet strong and ready for whatever the sea may throw at her. Then you notice the carved figure has the body of a fish. The figurehead is a mermaid.

The ship has been wedged high on the rocks by the sea, pushed further and further onto land by each subsequent storm. Only the sturdiest of timbers remain intact. The deck has holes in it and the mast is only a stump. Where the rest of it has gone is a mystery.

You walk around the ship, studying it from every angle. How many gold coins were spilled into the sea when it came ashore, you wonder. How many unfound coins remain somewhere nearby today?

Maybe you should go for a snorkel and see if you can find any that have been missed by other treasure hunters over the years. Storms would constantly churn up the sand on the seabed, who knows what treasure might have been uncovered in the last big blow.

You strip down to your bathing suit and grab your snorkel. But then as you reach the seaward side of the wreck and look back at the island, you notice a ladder made from two long wooden poles leaning against the cliff. Smaller branches are lashed to the main supports with vines to create steps. The ladder looks old and disused. Many of the rungs are missing. It looks like it's been rotting away for years.

A gull screeches, above the old wreck. You like the idea of diving for coins, but you also wonder how safe it is. Maybe you should go and explore the interior instead.

It is time for you to make a decision. Do you:

Go snorkeling by the shipwreck? **P91**

Or

Go back to the beach and explore the islands interior? **P88**

You have decided to go inland and explore the island.

The plan is to explore the interior of the island. Maybe you can even get to the summit. There could be all sorts of interesting things to find along the way.

When you reach the top of the beach, you pull back a palm frond and step into the jungle.

You stop for a moment and listen. You wonder what creatures live here. You can hear parrots squawking and the whoop, whoop, whoop, of some larger bird flying through the canopy high above.

You look around trying to decide which way to go. Everything looks similar.

Then you see a natural path leading slightly uphill towards the centre of the island. The path looks like it acts as a watercourse when the heavy tropical rains come. The ground has been washed clean of dirt, and you find yourself walking on a layer of pebbles, occasionally stepping around large boulders that block your way as you climb.

Some of the pebbles are almost clear. Quartz you figure. Then others appear that are amber in color. Then a glassy looking stone of pink appears.

You reach down to pick it up and hold it up to the light. You can see right through it. You remember reading about rose quartz, but you've never seen a piece so large or so perfectly round before.

You pop the rock into your daypack and dig around with the toe of your shoe to see if you can unearth any more. Each time you rake the pebbles in the watercourse over, more colored stones appear. All of them have glittering quartz in them. Some are a smoky grey and have a stripe of white running down their centers. Others are a pale green. You select a few of each color and tuck them away for safe keeping.

When you see two fist-sized chalky white rocks similar to ones you've seen before, you pick them up and hold them together.

Then you rub them together as fast as you can. Sure enough, little sparks of light are generated by the friction. You remember the name of this cool phenomenon. Triboluminescence. Now there's a word that will impress your family when you show them the rocks later on.

You put the two white stones together with the others you've collected into your daypack and start walking uphill again. Before you go very far, you come across a large pile of rocks.

On top of the cairn is a flat rock with a compass rose and an arrow engraved on it. The arrow points away from the natural pebble path and towards two large trees up the slope to your right.

Why the arrow is pointing you to steeper ground you're not quite sure. It is a far more difficult route to the top of the island than following the watercourse.

What should you do?

It is time for you to make a decision. Do you:

Carry on up the watercourse? **P98**

Or

Follow the arrow and go up between the two trees?
P100

You have decided to go snorkeling by the shipwreck.

You walk down to the water's edge and strip down to your bathing suit. You leave your pack sitting on the rocks and look for a safe place to enter the water. There is a wide channel with a sandy bottom between the rocks that you think might be a good place to start your search. After finding a good spot you put on your snorkel and ease yourself into the water.

The water is nice and refreshing after your walk around the rocks. Visibility is excellent and you can see many small fish darting back and forth. Rock walls hem you in on either side. From a big crack in the rocks, an orange lobster looks back at you. Its beady eyes follow you nervously as you glide past.

Every hole and crevice seems to be home to some creature or other. Urchins with sharp red spines are scattered across the bottom.

You take a deep breath and head down to the bottom, looking back and forth for anything interesting as you go. When your lungs begin to burn, you make for the surface to catch your breath.

With each dive you move further away from the island. After a number of unsuccessful dives, you decide to turn and head back towards shore. You are almost back to where you started, when something catches your eye.

You take a deep breath and head down once more. Then you see it again, wedged into a crack in the rock. It looks like a handle of some sort.

You grab on to the handle and pull. As you kick towards the surface, a short, slightly curved steel blade slides out of the narrow crack in the rock. You realize you've found a pirate's cutlass or 'machete' as they are called here in the Caribbean.

It is a beautiful sword. Inset into its silver handle are a number of gemstones. One glistens green, another red, and yet another amber. Holding tight to your find, you kick towards shore, eager to have a good look at your discovery.

After climbing back onto the rocks, you inspect the blade a little closer. It is remarkably clean. It's strange that something that had been submerged under the water for any length of time is so new looking, especially here in the tropics where the marine life grows so quickly. You would have thought it would have been encrusted with barnacles, algae and other sea life.

You hold the blade up to the sun. Beams of light reflect off the shining steel. Then you feel the cutlass begin to hum. When you tighten your grip on the handle, the blade vibrates even more. The hum turns to a high-pitched ringing as the blade vibrates faster and faster.

A big spark flashes from the end of the blade and you are knocked to the ground as the cutlass clatters onto the rocks.

"Ouch!" you say, rubbing your hand. What sort of strange cutlass is this?

You have seen pictures of similar swords in pirate books you've read, but you've never heard of one giving someone an electric shock before!

"That was so random," you mumble.

Afraid to pick up the cutlass with your bare hand, you dig into your pack and pull out your sweatshirt. Using it as insulation you carefully pick up the blade and wrap it up in the sweatshirt before placing it inside your pack for safekeeping.

The treasure hunting is going well so far, even if what you are finding is a little odd. If you want to do more exploring, it is time for you to make a decision. Do you:

Go back to the beach where you landed and go inland to explore more of the island? **P88**

Or

Climb the pole ladder? **P94**

You have decided to climb up the pole ladder.

Upon closer inspection the ladder looks quite sturdy. It is made from two long wooden poles with stout branches lashed between as steps.

Just to be safe you take the first few steps carefully, not sure if the old lashings will hold your weight, but after the first couple of steps you are quite confident that it is safe.

When you are about half way up the ladder, you hear what sounds like men singing. You wonder where they could have come from.

When you turn your head around to see who it is making all the noise, you are so shocked at what you see you nearly fall.

On the deck of the wrecked ship are a group of men dressed in long black shorts and striped shirts of varying colors. A few of the men have scarves tied around their heads.

One of the men wears white pants, high black boots and a jacket with tails. He has a black hat on his head and holds a cutlass in his hand like the one you found.

Many of the men hold tankards in their hands and are drinking and singing.

You can't believe your eyes. What are these men doing here? Are they ghosts? You wonder if the vibrating cutlass has caused you to go through a time-warp somehow. Why are the men dressed so strangely? Nobody dresses like that anymore, except people going to a costume party.

Unsure of what is happening, you climb the ladder as quickly as you can, hoping the men don't see you. When you reach the top of the ladder you hide behind a bush and watch.

Once the men finish their tankards, a couple of them bring a chest up from the ship's hold. The man with the cutlass is yelling orders. You hear the sailors yell.

"Aye aye Captain!"

The wrecked ship doesn't look as damaged for some reason. And it's only just on the rocks, not way up like it was before.

The mast is back too, and from it flies a Spanish flag of red and gold. You shake your head and wonder what is going on here. This can't be happening!

Then you see the gold and red flag drop to the deck and a black and white skull and crossbones go up in its place. The pirates have taken the ship. But how? All this happened years ago!

Six of the men lower a wooden rowboat over the side of the ship and climb down some rope netting into it. The other men then carefully lower the trunk down to them. Once the trunk is safely stowed in the bottom of the boat and the oars readied, the men in the boat row off around the island.

Where are they going? Is there treasure in that trunk?

When a loud boom sounds, you look back towards the

mainland and see smoke coming from the walls of the fortress.

What is going on? Someone is shooting the old cannon on the wall. How can that be? You notice the tower on one end of the fortress is still intact.

But that's impossible!

Then a series of massive booms sound behind you. They must be coming from the far side of the island. Seconds later, part of the fortress wall is smashed in by cannon balls smacking against it. Men in the fortress are running around like busy ants behind the walls.

There is another BOOM and two Spanish ships at anchorage in the calm waters below the fort burst into flames. Spanish sailors are jumping into the sea to escape the fire.

You don't know how it is possible, but somehow you've ended up in the middle of a battle.

Is the cutlass you found magic? You look again at the cutlass in the hand of the captain on the wrecked ship. The handle glitters green, red and amber just like the one you found.

More flashes appear on the fortress walls and you hear the scream of a cannonball overhead. One cannonball crashes into the trees nearby, breaking branches and sending a flock of birds squawking as they fly off in alarm. Another flurry of shots from the fortress smash into the deck of the wrecked ship and some of the pirates go flying.

It is time for you to make a decision. Do you:

Walk around the island and continue to watch the pirates in the row boat? **P118**

Or

Stay where you are and keep watching the pirates? **P124**

You have decided to carry on up the watercourse.

You have decided to ignore the arrow pointing you up towards the steeper part of the slope and continue along the easier and less steep watercourse that leads up the centre of the valley. You've been making good time and can't see any reason to change your strategy. The watercourse is easy to climb apart from when you need to work your way around the occasional large rock blocking your way.

The creatures on the little island don't seem afraid of you as you go along. Maybe they haven't seen many people before. One little bird is flitting quite close by, almost following your footsteps. The bird has a fat body and a tail shaped like a fan. It nips around with remarkable speed nabbing tasty morsels. Then you realize the bird is hunting all the insects that you have disturbed.

As you progress further up the path, the ground starts to rise sharply and more big rocks start to block your path, making the climb more difficult.

As you move around one of the boulders in your way a sound further up the hillside attracts your attention. You stop walking and listen. The noise is getting closer.

A large cracking sound startles you. Whatever it is coming down the hill towards you is moving fast. Could it be an animal of some sort, or is it something else? You crouch down, dropping to one knee and try to see under the branches blocking your view.

When you see the tumbling boulder, it is too late for you to move out of its way.

It is coming right at you. You scream. In the split second before it hits, you have the sudden realization that the arrow on the cairn was trying to warn you of rock falls!

Unfortunately this part of your story is over.

You decided to continue up the watercourse. Those boulders blocking the path further down the hillside, should have given you a clue that this is an unstable area. Avalanches and rock falls often run down the centre of gullies like this one.

It is time for you to make a decision. Do you:

Make that last decision differently? **P100**

Or

Go back to the very beginning of the story? **P1**

You have decided to follow the arrow and go up between the two trees.

Whoever bothered to build this cairn of stones probably did so for a reason, so you decide to head up between the two large trees and see where it takes you. You're not very far up the slope when you hear a crashing sound flying down the hillside from above.

You crouch down and try to see under the branches. What is making all the noise? Then you realize it's a rock slide. A big rock from higher up has been dislodged and is coming down the hillside along the path of the dry watercourse.

A flash of grey the size of a car zips past you. The sound of branches breaking and the rumble of smaller rocks being loosened fill the small valley.

Had you decided to continue on up the watercourse, you would have been squashed like a bug.

You are shaking a little. That was too close for comfort. You sit down with your feet tucked under you and listen to the sounds crashing further down the valley.

Determined to get to the top of the island, you get up and move off. The slope is steeper here, but at least there isn't quite as much undergrowth and you've got tree branches to pull yourself up with.

Before long you reach a grassy patch of level ground. Growing in the middle of the meadow is a huge tree dripping with oranges. You can't believe your eyes. Never before have you seen such a big tree laden with so much fruit.

You pluck an orange from a low-hanging branch and start peeling off the skin. Then you break the orange into sections and pop one in your mouth. When you bite into it, juice runs down your chin and the orange flavor bursts into your mouth. This has got to be the tastiest orange you've ever eaten.

You wonder why it is here on the island, and why it is the only tree in the little meadow. You also wonder how anything could taste so delicious. Did pirates plant the tree here so they could pick the fruit to prevent scurvy from a lack of vitamin C? The tree looks old, but could it be that old? Maybe one of the villagers put it here. You must remember to ask the village boy when you get back to the mainland.

After finishing the orange and picking two more and putting them into your backpack for later, you look around wondering which way to go from here. You remember your math teacher telling you that the shortest distance between two points is a straight line, so you point your nose towards the top of the hill and start walking.

Once you've left the meadow, the ground gets steep quite quickly. Loose stones underfoot mean you have to pick where to step carefully. Sometimes your foot slips so you have to move quickly to regain your balance.

Finally the ground becomes less steep and you have the feeling the top is just over the next rise. Then you hear the sound of hundreds of birds. You must be close now.

After climbing up one last slope, you see the ocean. When you look out at the endless expanse of water it feels like you've come to the edge of the world.

Birds swarm in the sky. There are so many of them you wonder how they manage not to have mid-air collisions. A couple swoop down to check you out, screeching at you for invading their territory. Others are diving into the sea below, catching fish for their young ones back in their nests in the cliffs.

The ocean sparkles with a million pinpoints of light. A small patch of cloud far out to sea billows up like cotton wool but its underside is dark and flat. Rain falls in streaks from its grey bottom, but the rest of the sky is clear and sunny.

You are up high enough to see the slight curvature of the earth on the horizon as it stretches off in both directions. Seeing this curve reminds you that you are standing on a sphere that orbits around a sun in a solar system that is in a tiny part of a much larger Milky Way galaxy hurtling through space. It makes you feel incredibly small in one way, yet up here so high, you also feel like a giant.

You are about to sit down and rest for a moment, but before you do, you want to check out the strange looking structure that sits a few paces back from the edge of the cliff on the highest point of ground. It looks as though it has been here for quite some time.

The structure is a three-legged tower. The legs of the tower are spaced wide at the bottom and joined together at the top like a Native American tepee. Timber poles are lashed between each of its legs adding stability to the structure. A narrow ladder goes from the ground to a small lookout platform about three quarters of the way up.

A pair of old wood and iron pulleys hang from chains looped around the timbers. A rope runs from one pulley through to the other and then its end disappears over the edge of the cliff.

You are surprised you didn't see the tower from the water when you sailed around the island, but then the tower is set back from the edge a little, leaving only the length of rope to be spotted from below.

You walk around the structure looking at the placement of the pulleys. They look like they are for lifting things up from the water below. Like a primitive crane of sorts, but why here?

You walk towards where the rope is hanging over the edge of the cliff to check it out. A few paces away from the edge you get down on to your hands and knees and crawl carefully forward. As you near the edge you lay on your belly and inch forward and peer over the edge.

The view straight down makes your stomach lurch. There is nothing below but water.

Looking straight down from such a height makes you a little dizzy. The clearness and depth of the water makes the distance to the surface look even greater than it is. You grab onto the rope for security, just in case.

It is just as well, because the ground under you is rumbling.

"Earthquake!" you yell out as you push yourself back from the edge. But it is already too late. The edge of the cliff is breaking away. You twist the rope around your wrist and hang on as tight as you can, hoping that the rope will be strong enough to hold your weight.

As the edge of the cliff cracks way, the old rope creaks a little but thankfully, it doesn't look in any danger of breaking. Before you know it, you are hanging over the water far below.

You wrap one leg around the rope to ease the stress on your arm and hang on for dear life as the breeze swings you back and forth. Gradually the swinging stops and you try to pull yourself up a little at a time. It is hard work, and before long your arms are getting tired.

You are considering letting go and taking the plunge into the sea when you feel the rope begin to rise. You look up and hold on even tighter.

Then you hear a voice from above. "Hang on."

Slowly you start to rise. When your head reaches the

top of the cliff, you see a boy from the village over by the tower pulling on the rope.

Before you know it, you are over the edge and back on firm ground. The boy ties the rope around part of the wooden frame and comes over to where you are lying on the ground.

You sit up, shake your aching arms, and look up at the boy. "Wow that was close. What are you doing out here?"

"When I saw you sailing towards the island I decided to take my father's boat out and join you. I thought you might like a friend to help you look for treasure."

"That would be great," you say. "After my close calls today, I think it will be a lot safer exploring with someone else."

"Calls?" the boy asks. "You mean this isn't the first trouble you've been in today?"

You tell him about the rock fall.

The boy smiles at you. "Sounds like you need a minder."

The two of you have a good laugh and then the boy reaches his hand out and helps pull you to your feet.

"You're probably right," you say still holding his hand. "What's your name?"

"It's Kai," says the boy and you solemnly shake as you swap names.

"So what should we do?" asks Kai.

"I don't know. Maybe we should climb up the tower

and see if we can spot something interesting from up there?"

"Or, we could go back down to the beach and go exploring around the island in my father's boat," Kai says.

It is time for you to make a decision. Do you:

Climb the tower? **P107**

Or

Go exploring in Kai's father's boat? **P126**

You have decided to climb the tower.

After walking over to the tower, you approach the narrow ladder that leads up to the observation platform. You should both get an excellent view of the island and surrounding ocean from way up there.

Kai runs over and starts climbing. He's quick. You figure it's probably all the practice he's had climbing coconut trees.

"Hurry up," he says as races up.

You take the climb a little slower, preferring to get there in one piece rather than rush.

After the climb, the two of you find yourselves standing on the platform looking out over the surrounding jungle and ocean.

The warm ocean breeze blows through your hair.

As you suspected, the view from up here is amazing. Over the treetops and across the short stretch of water, you can see the walls of the old fortress. White spray crashes into the rocks below its crumbling walls.

Further to the left, the resort buildings nestle close together in a big U-shape around the aqua blue of the big swimming pool.

Then you see the thatched huts of the village.

"There's my house," Kai says pointing.

"Which one?" The huts blend into their surroundings so well, they are hard to spot. The villagers' fishing boats are little more than brightly colored dots on the beach.

The lighthouse looks small from this high up. Its red and white stripes make it look like a piece of Christmas candy.

"I can see a lot, but no obvious spot to hide treasure," you say.

"Me neither."

"So maybe you're right. Maybe this tower was just for the pirates to use when they were attacking the fortress."

You are about to climb down when you notice something lying in the long grass ten or so paces from the tower. The area is so overgrown that you almost missed it.

"What's that?" you say, pointing to a metal grid of some sort.

"I don't know, let's go down and take a look," Kai says as he swings his leg down and starts descending.

By the time you get down, he is pulling weeds from around the object.

"It's a metal basket of some sort," Kai says.

You help him clear the rest of the weeds around the basket and then the two of you sit it upright.

"Looks in pretty good shape," you say.

The basket is made from strips of metal woven together and attached to a slightly heavier iron rim. The diameter of the rim is a little bigger than your outstretched arms and comes up to your waist. Three lengths of chain are attached around the rim of the basket at one end and joined together with a big iron ring at the other.

"I bet the pirates used this to move things up and down the cliff," you say. "See how it works? You tie a rope around this big ring at the top here, and then raise and lower it using the pulleys attached to the tower."

"Wouldn't you need a lot of men to do that?" Kai asks.

"No, you see the pulley's gearing makes it easy. The good thing is you'd only need one person if the rope is long enough because you can operate the pulleys while you're in the basket."

"How?" Kai asks.

It's not the easiest thing to explain, but you give it a go. "The rope is attached to the top of the basket. Then it goes around the pulleys which take all the weight. Then it comes back to you in the basket."

"I see," Kai says, studying the apparatus. "And then when you want to come up again you just pull on the rope and up you come. Right?"

"Right," you say. "Tie the loose end of the rope onto the basket whenever you want to stop, and you just hang there."

"Wow," the village boy says. "That sounds like fun!"

"It could be dangerous," you tell him.

Kai looks at you and smiles. "We could always go exploring in my father's boat if you're afraid."

You're not sure if you are afraid or excited.

"What do you think Kai?"

He smiles. "At least if we fall we'll fall into the water."

You peer over the edge. It is a long way down. But then you've climbed all this way. What should you do?

It is time for you to make a decision. Do you:

Lower yourselves over the cliff? **P111**

Or

Go back down and explore around the island in Kai's father's boat instead? **P126**

You have decided to lower yourselves over the cliff.

After getting all the grass out of the metal basket, you and Kai roll it to the edge of the cliff nearest the tower. You run the thick rope through the big iron ring and tie a couple of knots to secure it. Then you tie an extra knot just to be safe.

The rope now runs from the top of the basket through two pulleys and then runs back to where you are standing. There is lots of rope left over so there should be enough to get you all the way down the cliff.

"Let's test it first okay? We'll lower the basket on its own before we try it with us in there."

"Good idea," he says.

The two of you maneuver the basket as close to the edge as possible.

"You grab the rope and I'll shove it over the edge," you say.

The boy stands back from the edge and lets out a little more rope as you push the bottom of the basket over the edge.

"Okay, it's over," you say.

Kai starts lowering the basket.

You watch the basket's progress as it drops towards the sparkling water below.

After a couple of minutes, you yell out. "Okay, I think that's far enough. Let's see how hard it is to pull it back up again."

Kai starts pulling in the rope. "Hey it's easy, just like you said," he says. "Hardly heavy at all."

You grab onto the rope and help pull. The basket comes up surprisingly fast with both of you pulling. Before you know it, the rim of the basket is level with the edge of the cliff.

"Our turn," Kai says with a big grin.

You both take hold of the rope and creep forward on your backsides until your legs are dangling into the basket. Then with a quick look at each other, you both hop into the basket.

It sways a little but because you are both holding onto the rope it doesn't drop at all.

"Don't look down," you say. "And not too fast, it isn't a race okay."

Letting a little rope out at a time, the two of you lower yourselves down the side of the cliff. As you do, you pass by the nesting birds. The parent birds squawk in alarm as you pass, but refuse to leave their nests while you are there.

About a third of the way down the cliff you pass a narrow opening in the rock wall.

"Stop," you say. "I think I see something at the back of this hole."

You loop the rope around a big hook on the side of the basket and lean into the recess. The opening is narrow and covered in bird droppings, but it is big enough for you to crawl through.

"I wish we had a flashlight," Kai says.

Then you remember the lighter in your pocket and have an idea. You grab some dried grass and small twigs from a deserted bird's nest and squash it into a ball. Holding the lighter below the ball you flick the lighter. The ball catches fire immediately. Before long it is well alight.

You toss the ball into the opening. The light from the flame allows you to see a small chest hard up against the back wall of the tiny cave.

"Wow!" you say. "Look at that!"

Kai is speechless. His mouth is hanging open and his eyes are huge.

After double checking that the rope is well tied off, you climb over the rim of the basket across a narrow ledge and into the opening. You crawl past the burning ball towards the chest.

A solid clasp holds the lid of the chest closed, but there is no lock. You release the clasp and lift the lid.

When you see what is inside the chest your mouth opens wide too. You reach in and grab a handful of gold doubloons and hold them out for Kai to see.

"We've found it!" you cry out. "Look!"

"Yippee!" Kai yells. "But what now? How do we get it back to the mainland? It looks heavy."

You both think for a moment.

"I have an idea," you say. "Help me get the chest into the basket. Then we can both pull us up to the top. Then you get out and go down and get your father's boat and bring it around to this side of the island and wait below while I lower myself and the chest down into your boat."

Kai grins. "Aye aye, captain!"

The chest is pretty heavy, but the two of you manage to slide it out of the cave and down into the basket. Then the job of pulling the basket back up starts. The added weight of the chest has made the job harder, but with the two of you it only takes about ten minutes to get back to the top and tie off the rope.

"Right, I'll be back as soon as I can," Kai says as he climbs out.

While he's gone, you sit in the basket and enjoy the view. After a while the birds forget you are there. When you hear the steady putt-putt of a motor you look off to your left and see the boat coming around the headland.

You untie the rope and start your way down. Going down is a lot easier than it was going up.

The basket is nearly at water level by the time the boat is below you.

As Kai cuts the engine, he reaches up and grabs the basket to hold to boat in place while you pay out the last of the rope and climb out of the basket onto the deck. The boat sinks a little deeper in the water as it takes the additional weight.

After getting the chest out of the basket Kai grabs a rope and ties the chest down so it won't move about on the trip back to the village. Then he turns to you. "Alright, let's pick up your sailboat and I'll give you a tow back in. It will be much quicker."

"Wait. It might be better for me to take the basket back up and hide it at the top," you say. "We may not want people to know what we've discovered quite yet."

Kai nods. "Okay I'll meet you back on the beach by your sailboat."

You jump back into the basket and start pulling. Without the weight of the trunk, you make pretty quick progress. "See you soon," you yell down as the village boy motors off.

Once you're at the top, you untie the basket and roll it under some bushes. You pull the rope off the pulleys and hide that too. Then you head back down the way you came to the beach.

Kai is waiting for you when you arrive. You tie the bowline from your sailboat onto the back of his boat and jump aboard with him for the ride back to the mainland.

"So what are you going to do with your share of the treasure?" you ask.

"I'm going to get my father his operation to fix his eyes," he says.

You smile. "Then what?"

"And then depending how much money is left over, maybe I can buy the resort from its owners so the villagers can run it. We need jobs. Then I'd like to set up a school for the children."

"Buying the resort might take a lot of money," you say.

As you sail back, you think about the villagers and the lack of jobs and education.

"Hey I have an idea," you tell Kai. "Why don't you take all the treasure? That way you should have enough buy the resort."

Kai's eyes widens. "But what about your share? Half of it belongs to you."

You lift the lid and take a handful of coins from the top of the pile. "This will do me. I just need enough to buy my family a present each and that new computer I've had my eye on. Oh, there's just one condition."

"What's that?" Kai asks.

"You have to write and keep me up to date, until I can talk my family into coming back for another holiday."

"If I have anything to do with it, next time, your family's holiday will be free!" Kai says with a big grin.

You put the coins into your pocket. "Sounds like a good deal to me."

"Oh, and I want you to have this." The boy smiles and lifts the string of shells from around his neck. "These are cowry shells. In the old days my people used them instead of money. I want you to have them."

You take the necklace and place it around your neck. "Looks like we've found two sorts of treasure today," you say.

Kai nods his agreement. "You're right. Treasure is great, but friendship is the best treasure of all."

Congratulations! You've found the pirates treasure. This part of your story has come to an end.

It is time to make a decision. Would you like to:

Go back to the very beginning of the story? **P1**

Or

Go to the list of choices and start reading from a different part of the story? **P129**

You have decided to watch the men in the row boat.

You realize you are too close to the pirates raiding the Spanish ship. The men at the fortress have seen the pirates on deck and have turned one of their guns on them. You need to get out of the way before you get hit by a stray shot. You move behind a huge rock and wait for the Spanish to shoot again. Then, when they are reloading you can leave your shelter. When you hear three more booms, you make a run for it.

You run as fast as you can from one rock to the next. Each time the Spanish shoot, you move a bit further around, finding a place to shelter before the next barrage. By staying near the shoreline you can see the rowboat with the pirates and the chest as it makes its way around the little island.

The ground level is climbing as you go. The shoreline cliffs are getting steeper. At one point you have to use vines and branches to help put yourself up the hillside.

Before you know it, you're nearing the top of the island. You can see three pirate ships sitting behind the island firing their cannon over the hill towards the fort. At the top of the island, a man stands on a wooden tower waving flags, directing the pirate ships where to fire.

The pirates are faster at reloading their cannon than the Spanish and much more accurate. The pirates also have bigger targets. Both the Spanish ships and the fortress are larger than the quicker but smaller pirate raiders.

You've had to move inland a little and can no longer see the fortress between the trees. Nonetheless it is easy to hear the booms coming from both sides of the battle. Not many shots are coming from the fortress any more.

Near the top of the hill the jungle thins and the ground starts to level out. You can see the ocean through the trees again. The pirates in the rowing boat are making good speed. They've almost reached the headland. A few of the shots from the fortress come close to the rowboat, but then the pirates round the headland and gain protection from the island. When the spray settles, the men are pulling strongly on their oars. After the rowboat rounds the headland it disappears from view under the cliff.

Then suddenly the gun fire stops. It is so quiet, you can hear the birds and the slap of the waves on the hull of the pirate ships far below. It is dead quiet for nearly a minute. Then the pirates begin to cheer. The fortress has stopped firing. The pirates have won the battle.

The man in the tower is jumping up and down with glee. After a moment's celebration, he climbs down from his lookout post, grabs onto a rope and climbs into a metal basket hanging over the edge of the cliff. Using pulleys attached to the tower's strong timbers, he lowers himself towards the water below

You still can't see the rowboat and wonder why it

hasn't reappeared near the ships further out to sea.

You creep to the edge of the cliff on your hands and knees and peer over the edge. The basket is hanging just above the water. The pirates in the rowboat are lifting the trunk they took from the Spanish ship into the basket.

You wonder what they are doing. Then the man in the basket is joined by another from the boat and they start hauling on the rope, pulling the basket up again.

Should you run? Why are they bringing the trunk up to the top of the island?

Then you notice the basket has stopped rising. Instead, it hangs beside the sheer cliff. You see the two men lift the trunk out of the basket and push it into the side of the hill.

You wonder if when you get home to the future, there is any chance that the trunk will still be there. But to find that out, first you have to get back to the right time, back to your family and not this crazy place you've found yourself in, but how?

You think hard about your situation. You're pretty sure that the cutlass you found by the wrecked ship has something to do with it.

You are a bit scared, but you are determined to get back to your family. You take off your pack and take out the cutlass and lay it on the ground.

Carefully you fold back the sweatshirt exposing the sword. You stand back, but nothing happens. Maybe the magic only works when someone is holding the cutlass up?

Your hand trembles a little when you pick up the cutlass. Last time you held it you were knocked off your feet. A little afraid, you hold the sword as far from your face as possible.

The vibration starts as a quiet hum. Slowly it gains speed. Before long the cutlass is moving back and forth so fast it is only a blur and a high-pitched sound surrounds you. But before the cutlass knocks you down, you throw it as hard as you can over the cliff.

The sword is halfway to the water when there is a blinding flash. When you are able to see again, the pirate ships are gone.

You walk towards the edge of the cliff to where the rope is hanging over the side, get down on to your hands and knees and crawl carefully forward. As you near the edge you lay on your belly and inch forward.

The view down makes your stomach lurch. All you see is a dangling rope running down the sheer cliff. Where have the men gone? Are you back in the present?

The clearness and depth of the water, makes the distance to its surface look even greater than it is. The height makes you a little dizzy. As you look down you grab onto the rope for security, just in case.

It is just as well you did because the ground under you has been weakened by recent rain. Suddenly you feel the earth beneath you start to rumble. You push yourself back from the edge but it is already too late. The edge of the cliff is breaking away. You twist the rope around your wrist and hang on tight, hoping that it will be strong enough to hold your weight.

As the ground gives way, the rope creaks and stretches, but doesn't break. You swing back and forth over the edge in the slight breeze.

You wrap one leg around the rope to ease the stress on your arm and hang on for dear life as you dangle over the water far below. Gradually the swinging stops and you try to pull yourself up a little at a time, but it is hard work, and your arms are getting tired.

You are considering letting go and taking the plunge into the sea when you feel the rope begin to rise. You hold on even tighter.

Then you hear a voice from above. 'Hang on!'

Slowly you start to rise. When your head reaches the top of the cliff, you see the village boy standing by the tower, pulling the rope through a series of pulleys.

Before you know it, you are back on safe ground. The boy hooks the rope around a cleat on the frame of the tower and comes over to where you are lying on the ground.

You sit up and look up at the boy. "Wow that was close. What are you doing out here?"

"When I saw you sailing towards the island I decided to

take my father's boat out and join you. I thought you might like a friend to help you look for treasure."

"That would be great," you say. "I think it will be a lot safer exploring with someone else."

The boy smiles. "You're probably right. So where should we look first?"

"I don't know. Maybe we should climb up the tower and see if we can spot something interesting from up there?" you say.

"Or we could go back to the beach and go exploring in my father's boat," the boy says. "My name's Kai by the way."

It is time for you to make a decision. Do you:

Climb the tower? **P107**

Or

Go exploring in Kai's father's boat? **P126**

You have decided to stay where you are and keep watching the pirates.

The battle is raging. The fortress is firing their cannon as quickly as they can reload, but the Spanish are fighting a losing battle.

One of the pirate's shots hits the top of the turret on one end of the fortress wall, taking off its roof. Others smack into the various walls breaching them.

The fortress is beginning to crumble from the vicious attack.

One of the Spanish ships is sinking. Its mast is broken and men are swimming for shore.

When the fire reaches the powder kegs, the ship explodes sending flames and splintered timbers shooting off in every direction. The burning timbers hiss as they sink below the water.

You see more puffs of smoke from the fortress wall. The Spanish are still fighting despite the odds being against them. It has taken the men in the fortress a while to figure out where the pirate ships are shooting from.

Some of the Spanish turn their guns on the pirates looting the ship on the rocks just below your position. The old guns aren't very accurate, and unfortunately as the gunners on the fort take one of their last shots, you are in the wrong place at the wrong time.

You never see the cannonball coming.

Unfortunately you've been hit by a cannonball and this part of your story is over.

It is time for you to make a decision. Do you:

Go back to the very beginning of the story? **P1**

Or

Make that last choice differently? **P118**

You have decided to go exploring in Kai's father's boat.

You and Kai have taken the safe option. You have decided to go back down to the beach and take his father's boat out exploring around the island a little more.

The two of you have lots of fun diving at different spots around the little island, but unfortunately you don't find any more treasure. This is a real shame because the boy and his family could really do with the money that finding the treasure would bring.

The boy explains how his father is unable to fish because of the cataracts on his eyes, and the only thing the family has to live on is the fish he can catch, the vegetables his mother grows, and a few dollars his aunty makes working at the resort.

"How much would it cost to fix your father's eyes?" you ask him.

"More than we'll ever have," the boy replies.

You think about this as the two of you sail back to the mainland. Kai's story makes you realize how much you have compared to him. After all, your family can afford to take overseas holidays to exotic places and eat fancy food and swim in fancy pools. Kai's family is struggling just to put food on the table.

When you get back to the beach by the resort, you are about to say goodbye to your new friend. Then you have an idea. You reach into your pocket and then hold out your palm towards the village boy. In the middle of your hand sits a gold doubloon.

"Here you go. I found this near your village. You should take it and use the money for your father's operation. It only seems fair."

The boy's eyes light up when he sees the coin. "But that's gold. It must be worth—"

"Please take it," you insist. "I only ask one thing in return."

"Sure," Kai says. "Anything."

"Send me a postcard from time to time … until I can talk my family into coming here on holiday again."

The boy smiles and lifts the string of shells from around his neck. "These are cowry shells. In the old days my people used them instead of money. I want you to have them."

He takes the necklace and place it around your neck.

Then, you drop the coin into his hand. "Looks like we've both found treasure after all," you say.

Congratulations! You've found some treasure. But is there more if you take another path?

Have you explored the old Spanish fort and been out to the lighthouse? Have you climbed the big tree?

Who knows what adventures you might find.

This part of your story has come to an end. But there

are still decisions to make. Do you want to:

Go back and try a different path? **P1**

Or

Go back and find out what happens if you lower yourself over the cliff? **P111**

Or

Go to the list of choices and start reading from another part of the story? **P129**

List of Choices

(continued next page)

More You Say Which Way Adventures.

Lost In Lion Country

Between the Stars

Danger on Dolphin Island

In the Magician's House

Secrets of Glass Mountain

Volcano of Fire

Once Upon an Island

The Sorcerer's Maze - Adventure Quiz

The Sorcerer's Maze - Jungle Trek

YouSayWhichWay.com

13268966R00081

Printed in Great Britain
by Amazon